THE STEIN REPORT

THE STEIN REPORT

JOSÉ CARLOS LLOP

*Translated from the Spanish by
Howard Curtis*

Hispabooks
Publishing

Hispabooks Publishing, S. L.
Madrid, Spain
www.hispabooks.com

Originally published in Spain as *El informe Stein* by
    Muchnick, 1995 / RBA, 2008
First published in English by Hispabooks, 2014
English translation copyright © by Howard Curtis
Design and Illustration © Simonpates - www.patesy.com

A CIP record for this book is available from the British Library

ISBN 978-84-942284-1-4 (trade paperback)
ISBN 978-84-942284-2-1 (ebook)
Legal Deposit: M-5125-2014

This novel is for H. and our two children, for that summer of 1994
I spent on the island of Neverland, writing it.

Or watch the things you gave your life to, broken,
And stoop and build 'em up with worn-out tools.

1

Guillermo Stein came to the school in the middle of the year, arriving on a bicycle. None of us came to school by bicycle.

Guillermo Stein's bicycle was an Italian bicycle, black in color and very high. You would hardly have seen him over his bicycle, this newcomer Stein, if he hadn't been wearing a red rain cape over his shoulders, tied at the neck, off which the raindrops slid onto the ground. Because that was the year it rained all it ever could, when it didn't stop raining throughout the school year. That was why none of us came to school by bicycle. Beneath the line of umbrellas we saw Guillermo Stein arrive: we saw his back sheathed in that red cape and, beside the lamp on the rear mud guard, a white oval plate with two black letters—CD—and a coat of arms with a Latin motto and unicorns and fleurs-de-lys. Guillermo Stein had come to school on a bicycle that belonged to the diplomatic corps of a nation whose coat of arms did not appear in the atlas.

But that wasn't the only unusual thing about the arrival of Stein. It was about the time when Guillermo Stein arrived at the school that Father Azcárate died. Of apoplexy. The word echoed through the cloisters and courtyards and classrooms. To us, apoplexy was a sign of the wrath of God, the word itself had a sinister tinge, as if describing a sea monster. We still remembered the dead man's diatribes against Luther, who was one of his scholastic obsessions. We remembered the way his eyes had bulged from their sockets whenever he described the symptoms of Luther's illness. A-po-ple-xy, he would intone angrily from the platform, while we all prayed in silence that, when the hour of our death arrived, it would not be as a result of this Lutheran plague.

Luther and Stein; apoplexy and the red rain cape; the rain and that coat of arms that was nowhere to be found in the pages of the atlas, where all the coats of arms were displayed like exotic butterflies pinned in the boxes of a collector.

"A bad omen," Palou said. "I wouldn't be surprised if we ended up failing. Stein is a strange character and I don't like strange characters. They throw things off balance."

Palou was our class captain. Palou was strong and shrewd and he led us from the shadows, with the kind of impunity possessed only by those who are strong and shrewd at the same time. Palou's classification was a bad beginning for Stein. To Palou, balance was the key to life, a natural balance of which only he had the measure: to Palou, it was terrible to throw things off balance, something to be condemned for without benefit of trial.

The morning Stein arrived, it was my group's turn to keep vigil over Father Azcárate's body. When Father Laval, the prefect of our year, told us the day's order, a vague, silent tension gripped us at our desks—except for Stein, who remained absorbed in his own thoughts, as if he were exploring the jungles of that nation whose coat of arms did not appear in the atlas. None of us liked to keep vigil over the dead in the school's crypt. Over any dead man, but especially Father Azcárate: we were afraid that his illness had left marks on the waxen face of his corpse, and imagined Luther's anguish clearly visible on the lips and eyes of the body over which we were about to keep vigil.

The vigil lasted twenty-four hours, with groups of seven, led by the consuls of the various subjects, doing half-hour shifts. This funeral rite was conducted by those of us who had already turned eleven but not yet sixteen. It was a custom of the school, one intended to form our characters and to bring home to us that life was but a fleeting dream. I was consul of history and my group was given the first shift: the worst, because the dead man might not be dead, he might suddenly open his eyes, struggle with the shroud in an attempt to climb out of the coffin. Even if he was dead, we knew that he could hear us, we had known that ever since, during our spiritual exercises, Father Riche had told us, grim-voiced, how death is merely apparent and how at first the dead, even though they are dead, still hear everything that is happening in the world of the living. The question was whether the dead also guessed what was going on in the minds of the living. If so we were doomed, because as we kept vigil over Father Azcárate's body, we were all thinking about Luther—or, worse still, about what sins Father Azcárate could possibly have committed for God to have punished him with the same illness and death as that heretic.

I said "all," but I was wrong, I made the mistake that is common when the usual balance is upset: the mistake of forgetting. I forgot Stein. Stein was in my group, just to the left of Father Azcárate's face, directly opposite me. Guillermo Stein did not look at Father Azcárate, even for a few seconds. He was looking at us, observing us just as we would observe the amoeba and paramecia in the science lab. As if the six other members of the funeral bodyguard were amoeba and paramecia and Father Azcárate were as invisible as the lens of a microscope.

When our shift was over, we were relieved by the next group. Palou was the consul of mathematics and as we performed the changing of the guard—a maneuver that required doing an about-turn in a fixed position, something between a gymnastic display and a military parade—he questioned me with his eyes about Stein, as one might question a fellow pupil about the fermentation of a rare species of grass in the middle of an exam. Furtively, I shrugged my shoulders, as cowards shrug their shoulders in the middle of an exam. Members of the community were kneeling on the prie-dieus, praying: black cassocks on red velvet in the flickering, suffocating yellow light of wax candles soaked in incense. Their bowed heads were a display of bald patches: from incipient crowns to full billiard balls. I never understood why priests start to lose the hair on the tops of the heads, nor did I notice any traces of the devil on Father Azcárate's face.

We went back up to the classroom in formation, while the rain lashed the cloister and spattered our clothes. Whenever one of the fathers died, the academic activities of the school were paralyzed for a day. Classes were suspended and those hours of work and rest were devoted to study and prayer—as well as that dreaded half-hour spent keeping guard in the crypt.

In that first study hour, Stein devoted himself to arranging his belongings in his desk. I kept an eye on him, watched how he introduced his things into the only private sanctuary that each of us possessed at the school. I was keeping an eye on him because of my curiosity, but also in order to have something to tell Palou when he got back from the crypt. Guillermo Stein had arrived on a bicycle belonging to some mysterious diplomatic corps, carrying a pigskin case with two flaps, held in place by buckles, at the front. It was more like a teacher's briefcase than a student's satchel, and had the map of Africa at the back: a dark stain, not a defect in the leather, but the result of carelessness, the spilling of a bottle of cologne, perhaps, or contact with fire. The map of Africa was clearly visible from my desk.

Stein opened the green lid, painted like the doors of a coach, and rested it against the line for inks and pencil. The hinges inside glittered in the dark. I was able to see some of Stein's belongings: 1) Three standard sized red exercise books. 2) Seven books bound in Prussian blue paper. 3) A metal Craven-A tobacco tin, as red as his cape with the head of a black cat surrounded by gilded lettering. 4) A sepia-colored group photograph full of plumes and gaiters, which he stuck to the inside of the desk lid with tacks. 5) A kaleidoscope. 6) A cigar box. 7) Another photograph with jagged white borders, which seemed to be the photograph of a woman dressed in a suit, and which he put inside one of his exercise books. 8) A Bakelite pen, a German pencil, and another one, intact and unsharpened, with two colors: blue and red. 9) A worn, cinnamon-colored crocodile-skin wallet.

When this operation was over, Stein carefully closed the desk, turned, and smiled at me. I smiled back, without shrugging my shoulders as cowards do and as I usually do when I don't know what to say, or how to respond.

From the platform, Father Laval started to recite the rosary out loud.

At home that evening, I mentioned Stein's arrival to my grandparents. I didn't live with my parents: I lived with my grandparents. My parents were always traveling. My parents were amber-colored postcards; my parents were black and white postcards machine-tinted in garish and unlikely colors, as garish and unlikely as the colors of the cellophane wrappers that candies come in. So my grandparents were my parents, even though they weren't my parents, and my parents were views of the Promenade des Anglais in Nice, or sailboats in the port of Marseille, or beach huts at San Juan de Luz, or the white cliffs of Dover, or little cafés in Cairo, Tangier or Alexandria. There were always lots of cafés and seaports and streets with djellabahs and donkeys or luxury automobiles in those rectangular images of my parents, which always had scribbled notes on the back in my mother's handwriting, messages that said hardly anything, just: this is a really nice place, I don't see much of your father, he's always working, take care of yourself, love, your parents.

We were having dinner in the smoking room. We always had dinner in the smoking room, beneath an alabaster lamp that gave off a light as yellow as the candles in the crypt. And we always had the radio on. My grandfather liked to have dinner with the radio on because at that hour they were usually broadcasting a piano recital.

"The piano facilitates digestion," my grandfather would say, "and refines feelings. A man has to look after his digestion and always keep his feelings refined. If he doesn't, he runs the risk of turning into an animal."

That was what my grandfather would say amidst the cascading of the notes from the piano, the grace before the meal, the French omelet, the bread spread with tomato, and the fruit. When I mentioned Stein's arrival, I was peeling an apple, a red apple with lines that were ocher-colored like the blotches on my grandfather's hands. My grandmother looked at my grandfather when I said the word Stein, and my grandfather adjusted his glasses when he heard the word Stein. For the first time, to me, the word Stein was like the hissing of a cobra, or the sound of a bullet before it hits its target. And I had the feeling that, to them, the word Stein sounded like something that can't be seen and which, precisely because it can't be seen, conceals a danger. That was why, to me, it was like the hissing of a cobra or the sound of a bullet before it hits its target.

They said nothing, and it struck me as strange that they said nothing, because my grandparents always talked to me about the families of other pupils and how they had met them and if they had farms or nice houses near the old walls of the city, facing the sea, or if any member of their family had been very ill, or had been wounded in the war and had been awarded a military cross, or if they were healthy as a horse and were dying precisely from being healthy as a horse. But they didn't say anything about Stein, as if that night's piano recital were more interesting than usual.

When I went to bed, there was lightning outside, and the flashes lit up my room as if it were day, but with a different light from the light of day, a light as intense as the crack of a whip or the fall of the bucket in the house cistern. I opened the cardboard box where I kept my parents' faces and, as I did every night, looked through my collection of postcards. I looked through them, but didn't read them, because I never read them. It was my grandmother who read them to me and as she finished her eyes would cloud over and change color, the way the water in a pond changes color when a cloud passes across the sun. That night I dreamed about Father Azcárate burning in the flames of hell and I woke in a sweat in the middle of the night, and saw the postcards at the foot of my bed because the lightning was still flashing and the whole room was lit up as if it were day, but with a light different from the light of day.

I haven't talked about Guillermo Stein's clothes. Guillermo Stein's clothes were like his cape or the oval plate on the rear mudguard of his bicycle. We didn't wear uniforms in our school, but we might as well have. We all had very fair complexions, we all smelled of the same cologne, and we all had parts in our hair, however short we wore it. Our sweaters were navy blue, gray or brown, the colors of partridge feathers, knitted at home by our mothers—except for mine, which were knitted by my grandmother. The buttons were leather and looked like tiny half soccer balls, and the pants were made out of our fathers' old pants—except for mine, which were made out of my grandfather's old pants, which meant that mine were older. They were knee-length and were also gray, blue or brown, the color of partridge feathers. White shirts and brown shoes. And striped smocks, each with a pocket over the left breast, and the school shield and our surname sewn into the pocket. We would wear the smocks when we went down into the courtyard.

Guillermo Stein did not have a smock. He arrived in the middle of the year and did not have a smock. And his sweaters, which had a much smaller weave and were better-made than ours, closed up to the neck with no buttons, weren't blue or gray or brown. Guillermo Stein wore sweaters that were red like his rain cape, green like the glass in olive oil bottles, or yellow like the stripes in the courtyard, like the stripes that marked the limits of the handball field where we played soccer. And he wore dark leather pants, with lots of pockets, strong pockets that were the envy of Palou. And even Stein's pants that weren't of leather had lots of pockets, as if Stein kept many things in his pockets, as if he had more things to keep than we did, and needed more pockets to carry his secret belongings, not just a white handkerchief like the rest of us.

Stein was blond and had blue eyes with copper flecks. None of us was blond. None of us had blue eyes with copper flecks.

"My father was a friend of Count Ciano and I'm a secret agent of His Holiness."

He said this without blinking, but also without looking us in the eyes. Palou was electrified. Palou was always electrified when he didn't have an answer to something. It was as if the lack of words sent an electric shock through him: his lower lip would quiver and his eyes would dissolve into a watery liquid that was not tears, no. It was the liquid exuded by the dead: Palou's eyes became like the eyes of dead fish. Because for Palou, the lack of response was like being dead; as he never tired of saying, "If you don't answer it's because you're dead." So I said, Why don't we call Planas?

Planas was our specialist on World War II. Planas knew everything there was to know about World War II. Planas had an uncle who had fought in Russia with the Blue Division. Planas's uncle was called Raimundo and had seen a lot of the world. He had carried the plans to General Muñoz Grandes, and when he died, in a hotel in Barcelona, the only belongings that the police found were his souvenirs of Russia: a Luger pistol and the Iron Cross. The truth is that they said they had found a suitcase full of forged banknotes and a number of boxes containing vials of penicillin. But in the newspaper they only mentioned the Luger pistol and the Iron Cross, as if a pistol and a medal could explain the mystery of Planas's uncle's death.

It had been Palou's idea to corner Stein in the gymnasium and ask who he was, where he was from, what schools he had studied in, why he had arrived in the middle of the year and why on a bicycle. Stein did not express any surprise: it was as if he had been waiting for us. "My father knew Count Ciano and I'm a secret agent of His Holiness." That was all he said. Without blinking or showing any kind of nervousness, but also without looking us in the eyes, as if he already knew the customs of this group of common protozoa that surrounded him. That was when I said, Why don't we call Planas?

The task of calling Planas fell to Rovira. Rovira was our messenger; he ran like the wind and was so small, he could go anywhere pretty much without being seen. Rovira was always smiling, displaying his big, horsy teeth. Planas, on the other hand, never smiled. He had hair as black as a raven and could recite, in order, the parts of a MG47 machine gun, the secret Resistance codes before the Normandy landings, the deployment of naval forces in Okinawa, or the tactics of the Wehrmacht in the Battle of the Bulge. Planas knew everything there was to know about World War II.

"What he said about Count Ciano is plausible," Planas said. "As for being a spy of his Holiness, I don't believe it. A candidate for camerlengo, at best. Uncle Raimundo also met Count Ciano on his trips to Rome with Serrano Súñer. My uncle told me Ciano was planning to make the island Italian. His plan, my uncle told me a few months before he died, was to turn Majorca into a military base and a place of rest and recreation for the Fascist top brass. But couldn't even win Abyssinia, where they were only up against spears . . ."

Planas spoke like someone declining in Latin. Planas always spoke as if he were in a Latin class, translating a passage from *The Gallic Wars* aloud, without smiling, barely moving a single muscle in his face, but with a strange light in his eyes, like the light that dervishes or Indian holy men have. We all listened to Planas as he talked and nobody asked him what this or that meant: camerlengo, for example. Planas had said camerlengo and we had all accepted it, thinking that perhaps the coat of arms on Stein's bicycle was the coat of arms of the camerlengos, although none of us had any real idea what the word camerlengo meant. But Planas had also said spy—spy and not secret agent, which was what Stein had said. And the word spy wiped from Palou's eyes that same whitish liquid that the eyes of dead fish have.

Planas's slip was enough for Palou: he was already quite pleased. Now he only had to wait. He already knew what Stein was: a spy. And if he wasn't a spy, his father must be, with that name, Stein, and Palou knew that he could insult Stein any time he wanted, at one of those moments Palou knew so well, when Stein dropped his guard and was just like one of us. Then Palou would show his worth, as he had always done, and would demonstrate to Stein why he, Palou, was the captain of our section and not somebody else, not Rovira, or Fortuny, or Calafat, or Orfila, or Dezcallar, or Casasnovas, or Prim, or Forteza, or Salom, or Planas, who was wiser than Palou, even though Palou was consul of mathematics, or me, but Palou, only Palou, and then Stein would know who Palou was and balance—Palou's balance—would be restored.

And Palou said to Planas, "I want to know everything there is to know about Stein's family. I want a written report on Stein's family." Because Palou knew that he wouldn't get anything out of Stein and that Planas would be able to find out all there was to find out, because Planas was wise and saw people as the characters in a novel he would never write.

"Bonet, you aren't even looking at the blackboard."

Father Puig's bluntness was a bluntness equaled only by the passion with which he expounded his subject. We sometimes thought Father Puig would die of heart failure up there on the platform, in mid-lesson. We imagined Father Puig foaming at the mouth and clawing at the air and his glasses falling to the floor in slow motion—falling to the floor but not breaking, because they had fallen in slow motion.

Father Puig was our religion teacher, and the passion with which he presented the history of the church councils, the decadence of the Rome of Augustus or the strategic skill of the Maccabees, made him sweat copiously and jump up and down on the platform or throw himself across the desk like a panther seeking out the ingratitude of his pupils, seeking out those of his pupils who did not appreciate the passion with which he explained what he called "the path by which all of you have had the privilege of coming this far."

Father Puig was a strategist who liked colored chalk. The plans of Biblical battles drawn on the blackboard were a marvel that would have been envied by Napoleon's general staff. We were fascinated by Father Puig's battle plans. For those three hours per week when we were taught by Father Puig, our lives became as colorful as Stein's sweaters. But they also hung from a thread, an invisible thread controlled by Father Puig's whims and manias and those handkerchieves with which he wiped his brow or hid his face, camouflaging himself the better to watch us, to watch us without being seen.

And so, after this maneuver with the handkerchief, and while the yellow, green, red or blue arrows on the blackboard and the mountain ranges and the strategic deployment of the archers all remained as motionless as a landscape after battle, his pieces fell, as his glasses fell in our imagination. One was Montaner; the other Bonet.

Bonet particularly liked Father Puig's classes. Bonet competed with Father Puig for our attention. Bonet would put his hands together to form a kind of telescope and whenever Father Puig turned his back to us, he would look at him through his telescope, and it really did seem as if Bonet was looking through a telescope and we had to make an effort not to laugh. And when Father Puig turned around to face us, Bonet would position his wristwatch in such a way that the light bounced off the face of Bonet's watch and it would look as if Father Puig had a crown of light above his head, as if he were a saint like those whose images hung on the walls of the sacristy and the background of the picture were a baroque landscape filled with symbols and the symbols were the elephants that fought in the battles of the Maccabees or a tree with the names of the holy fathers at the Council of Nicaea, where they conceded that women possessed a soul—a huge mistake, it seems to me, Father Puig always said.

"So, Bonet, you don't know on what flank Eliezer attacked the armies of Antiochus. So, Bonet, you have a telescope but you can't see further than your filthy nose, you snotty little brat. I'm giving you a zero grade for conduct, Bonet, and you know what a zero grade for conduct means: three of those and you're out of the school."

Bonet would smile silently, with a shy smile that struck Father Puig as defiant. Because an inappropriate smile was always a defiant smile.

"Bonet, you've just earned yourself another zero grade for conduct. If you ever grow up, Bonet, you'll be a money lender: you obviously like accumulating interest."

Then Bonet would pretend to shake—Bonet never shook except when he pretended to shake. "But why, Father?"

"For being like flypaper. For standing there with that stupid smile of yours as if catching flies. You're stupid, Bonet, and you're stupid for two reasons: for asking why and for being like flypaper. Now sit down and shut up, or else you may accumulate more interest and get a third zero."

And Bonet sat down very slowly, the way he always sat down, barely fitting behind his desk because he was so lanky, silently wishing Father Puig did not die on the platform because then Bonet wouldn't make his telescope, and to him the zero grades were like the sound of the rain beating on the windows: a normal occurrence during that year when Stein arrived. Bonet didn't give a damn about the zero grades because his father was the civil governor and he knew they would never expel him, however many zero grades he got and all he wanted was for Father Puig and his biblical armies to live for ever so we could see his face and his hands, like white birds' claws in the choir stalls of the school chapel beside the older Jesuits, those waiting for death in the choir stalls of the school chapel while the whole school followed the nine a.m. mass or attended a funeral, like Father Azcárate's, for example, when the voice of the rector sounded like a voice from beyond the grave, the voice of Father Azcárate, for example, after he suffered his final attack of apoplexy, the voice of Father Azcárate as he lay dressed in black and gold and shrouded in incense smoke.

My grandparents received visitors on Thursday evenings. On Thursday evenings visitors would come, and it seemed as if they had come equipped with a stopwatch, because every half-hour, from six o'clock on, the bell would ring in my grandparents' house. There were two bells in my grandparents' house: one was electric and sounded like the buzzing of an insect trapped in a glass jar, and the other was a little bell that tinkled like the one at the doors of the convents I visited with my grandmother at Christmas and Easter. And depending on whether it was the electric bell or the little bell that rang, I knew if the visitors were friends of my grandparents, or relatives like the old Viala sisters or my Uncle Federico, for example, who came every Thursday to see my grandparents, and only on Thursday, and I noticed that my grandparents were friendlier toward their friends, those who rang the electric bell that sounded like the buzzing of an insect, than toward my Uncle Federico, who pulled the ring hanging next to the heavy door of my grandparents' house that set the thin brass pipes in motion and made the little bell ring. Because toward the Viala sisters, my grandparents were as friendly as they were toward their friends.

On Thursday afternoon I didn't go to school, none of us went to school because one of the customs of the Jesuits was to close on Thursday afternoons, not on Saturday like the other schools. On Saturday afternoons we all went to school and the school was open, not like the other schools, which were closed on Saturday afternoons. I would open the house door on Thursday evenings, and my grandparents' friends usually brought me some gift or other: sugar candy, cutout soldiers or chocolate cigarettes. Except for the old Viala sisters, who brought me postcards because they knew that I collected the postcards my parents sent me, but what the old Viala sisters did not know was that I always threw theirs into the garbage in order not to confuse them with the ones from my parents, so that they didn't blur the outlines of those images of my parents. And the visitors smelled of camphor in winter and eau de cologne in summer.

And I would walk the visitors to the hall of the cornucopias, holding the pack of sugar candy in my hands or the cutout soldiers or the postcards or the chocolate cigarettes, and the hall of the cornucopias was hung with damask silk and on its walls were gilded cornucopias and a collection of fans in glass boxes, also gilded along the edges. I walked them to the hall of the cornucopias, where the doors to the balcony had been thrown wide open by my grandparents' maid, Eulalia, on Thursday morning while I was at school. Because visitors were never received in the living room where we spent our time or in the smoking room, which was my grandfather's favorite part of the house, but in the hall of the cornucopias, which was next to the library and remained closed for the rest of the week until Thursday morning arrived and Eulalia opened wide the windows to the balcony. And from six o'clock my grandparents would get up from the Isabelline armchairs where they had been sitting all afternoon and receive their visitors with smiles on their lips while the women would kiss each other and the men would pat each other on the back. And the visitors would sit down on one of the Isabelline couches and Eulalia would appear with a silver tray laden with cups of chocolate and Bohemian glass bottles of muscatel for the ladies and cognac and cigars for the gentlemen. And then I would go to my grandfather's library and wait for half an hour to pass and the bell to ring again and I would sit on one of the chairs upholstered in yellow and black velvet with mythological designs and cut out the cardboard soldiers, usually Queen Victoria's grenadiers, Carlist artillerymen or French hussars, or I would watch the rain and think that perhaps the bell would ring that evening and it wouldn't be either my Uncle Federico or the old Viala sisters, but my parents, and with them they'd have trunks covered in customs stamps and stickers from hotels in exotic cities because they were coming to stay and I would no longer have to go through my collection of postcards to know what my parents' true faces looked like at that time.

We all knew that Planas would write the report about Stein. Planas looked at people as if they were engravings in a science book, insects in a museum or the maps in the atlas where the coat of arms on Stein's bicycle did not appear. His approach was a methodical one, as methodical as Linnaeus's classification or the table of equivalents. And in addition, there was something that Planas didn't like and that was people talking about his Uncle

Raimundo behind his back. Not about his death in Barcelona, or about when he carried the plans to General Muñoz Grandes or met Count Ciano in the Villa Torlonia—no, those things were part of World War II, which was Planas's specialty, and Planas was proud of them. What Planas didn't like was people talking about his Uncle Raimundo's youth, a youth of wild nights, of gambling, of wrestling matches, a thuggish youth that would result in an Uncle Raimundo who was both hot-headed and cold blooded, with a black uniform and an itchy trigger finger, Palou had told us, but Planas didn't know that and was afraid that Palou would tell us about how itchy his Uncle Raimundo's trigger finger had been before his Uncle Raimundo fell from a horse, like St Paul on the road to Damascus, and said, I'm going to the Russian front, to be killed for my sins. But when he got to Russia he wasn't killed, the Bolshevik hordes could not defeat Planas's uncle, the one who carried the plans to General Muñoz Grandes, and Planas's uncle won the Iron Cross and came back without a single wound, but more wounded than if he had been wounded on the Russian front and more dead than if he had died, and that was why he went back to his old habits, which were the habits of the dead, until he was actually found dead in a hotel in Barcelona and there was talk of fake bank bills and boxes of penicillin, many boxes of penicillin piled up in the bathroom in that hotel in Barcelona, the Hotel Oriente it was called, Palou told us at recess, one evening when Planas was ill and didn't come to school and Palou took advantage of his absence to tell us the story of Uncle Raimundo, who had seen so much of the world.

Planas and I were friends. I was consul of history and he was our specialist on World War II, and perhaps that was why we were friends. We could talk about lots of things the others knew nothing about. And there was a kind of challenge between Planas and me, a friendly challenge: to see who got the most top honors year upon year. Planas and I usually had top honors almost every month, apart from a few distinctions if we caught the flu, for example, or we had laughed too much with Bonet when he was looking at Father Puig through his telescope. That was why I went with Planas to take a look at Guillermo Stein's desk, one afternoon when Guillermo Stein hadn't come to school and the others were in gym class in the gymnasium, which was where we had gym because it was impossible in the courtyard, given that it did nothing but rain in the courtyard, the year Stein arrived.

The first thing we saw when we opened Guillermo Stein's desk was a sepia-colored photograph stuck with thumbtacks to the underside of the green lid. I knew that photograph from having seen it in an issue of *Blanco y negro*, a magazine my grandfather had collected and bound before the war, when I wasn't even born and my mother was living with them and nobody knew anything yet about my father—as if anybody ever did know anything about my father. It was a photograph of European royalty, taken on the day of the funeral of King Edward VII of England. In the front row sat Alfonso XIII, George V and Frederick VIII of Denmark; and standing behind them were King Haakon VII of Norway, Ferdinand I of Bulgaria, Manuel II of Portugal, Kaiser Wilhelm II, George I of Greece, and Albert I of the Belgians. I knew that photograph by heart and I loved the polished gleam of the gaiters, the plumed helmets, the sabers and the decorations. I liked the King of Spain and King George of England, who was in the middle and looked to me like Tsar Nicolas II but at the bottom of the photograph it said: beside his Majesty the King of Spain is seated King George V of England, who I thought was the Tsar of all the Russias, and I assumed the editor of *Blanco y Negro* had made a mistake but then I thought: it isn't possible, the printed word is never wrong, that's why it is the printed word.

I recited to Planas the names of those in the photograph, which I already knew by heart from having looked at it so often in my grandfather's magazines and suddenly I became confused, suddenly I saw an unknown shadow between King George of Greece and King Albert of the Belgians, who was not looking at the camera but toward a corner of the room that could not be seen in the photograph, and that shadow was a face with a gummed mustache and a uniform with braids and stripes and silver and gold crosses and I knew that it did not belong to any European king and that face was as grave as the others but I knew he was an intruder and that there must be some kind of trick to the photograph and I said to Planas: maybe that's Stein's father and Planas replied: how strange, and just then Father Laval appeared, with his thick glasses, so thick that his eyes looked like those of a dragonfly, and he said to us "Very nice, Planas, very nice, Ridorsa, I never expected such a base act from you," and he slapped us both across the face and our faces burned as the torches must have burned in Westminster on the day of the royal funeral, the day that photograph was taken into which Stein's father had somehow snuck, and because of which neither Planas nor I got top honors that month, or a distinction, or even an honorable mention, because Father Laval gave us a four for conduct and the shame of it reminded me of Palou's crushing observation: I wouldn't be surprised if we ended up failing.

Father Laval looked like a German post office official. All Father Laval lacked was the green uniform. His glasses were like two minerals and his eyes were the size of a dragonfly's. At the end of the day, after reciting the rosary, Father Laval would read to us for half an hour or three quarters of an hour, because the day always ended with two hours of study and of those two hours of study, one belonged to Laval, what with the rosary and the reading. Father Laval would read us stories by Chesterton and stories by Kipling, and that half an hour or three quarters of an hour at the end of the day were the life that I wanted for myself when I became an adult and my grandparents' house became my parents' house.

Sometimes, when Father Laval read a story by Kipling or a passage from Chesterton, Stein would look at me and smile. He would turn to me and smile the way he had smiled when I watched him putting his things in his desk, and I saw his blue eyes with their copper-colored flecks smiling at me and I thought he was smiling at me because he didn't know that I had betrayed him by looking through his desk with Planas. And Stein seemed to realize that I wanted to live in a story by Kipling when I was older and I had the impression—when Stein turned to me and smiled—that he was already living in a story by Kipling or a passage by Chesterton even though he was no older than I was, no older than any of us, and I wondered how Stein had come to be a character from Kipling, how Stein had come to be a character from a novel. And one night, just before leaving school, while I was listening to Kipling's words in the voice of father Laval—"I fell into the hands of a Sergeant-Instructor of Machine Guns, by profession a designer of ladies' dresses"—and Stein was smiling at me, and I thought maybe Stein wanted to be my friend, as Planas was, and by being a friend of Stein I could also be a character from Kipling, living Stein's novel, before the years passed, the years that decide for themselves and force you into their pages, the way sailors were forced onto ships in the old days: press-ganged by bayonet-wielding soldiers of the king. So I became a friend of Stein's and after I became a friend of Stein's, I felt a vague fear, the kind of fear that some of Kipling's characters felt: fear of reprisals from Palou, if he came to suspect that I was a true friend of Stein's and not an ally helping Planas so that Planas could write his report about Stein. And I thought about my grandparents' silence when I told them that a new pupil had arrived whose name was Stein and the word Stein echoed through the smoking room like the hissing of a cobra, like the hissing of one of those cobras that appeared in the stories by Kipling that Father Laval read to us.

"Now pay attention, please. When you leave here, you're sure to hear about Hegel. What a bore that Hegel was, with all his abstruse, tasteless nonsense. Remember that people use Hegel to try and prove the non-existence of God. Well, you know what I'd do with all that Hegelian trash? I'd make a pile of his terrible books, light a match and set fire to them . . . What'll be left of Hegel then? Nothing, nothing will be left: just ashes, and ashes can't prove the existence or non-existence of anything at all. Don't listen to anyone who talks to you about Hegel when you leave here: you'll be bored. Because the people who talk about Hegel are boring people, coarse people with chips on their shoulders: throw the ashes at them and they'll run like rabbits, with their Hegel between their legs . . ."

Father Cristino was the only Jesuit in the college who we called by his first name, as if he were a Franciscan and not a Jesuit, a Brother instead of a Father: the Brothers were usually called by their first names, apart from Brother Loring, who taught us Latin and was a wise man who had refused to say mass out of humility, so they said, and it struck me that Brother Loring was a Tibetan lama who had decided to become a Jesuit, and when he laughed, Brother Loring's eyes narrowed like the eyes of a Tibetan lama. Father Cristino wore a monocle, an orange monocle, and had grey hair with green highlights. We all knew that those green highlights were caused by Father Cristino's cheap cologne, but we all said that Father Cristino's green hair had acquired that color because Father Cristino passed his hand over his nose before smoothing his hair. In class, Father Cristino would pass his hand over his nose before smoothing his grey hair with its green highlights.

Father Cristino said he had fought in the Civil War. He had a useless hand, did Father Cristino, a very small, thin, deformed hand, which he kept wrapped in a black cloth. It seemed to be made of red rubber, it looked like an orthopedic hand of red rubber. Father Cristino said his hand had been rendered useless while cutting some electrified barbed wire laid by the reds, some fiendish barbed wire manufactured in Czechoslovakia, Father Cristino said. But we all knew that Father Cristino's crippled hand had been crippled during his training, while trying to fix some kind of fuse on a high-tension pole. And we always asked him about his military campaign and about the Czech barbed wire and Father Cristino's face would light up and his green hair would stand on end and he would tell us about his heroic conduct during the war and we knew that Father Cristino was incapable of fighting in a war, incapable of going through barbed wire to kill the enemy, incapable of burning a book, even a book by boring old Hegel that demonstrated the non-existence of God.

Father Cristino was our philosophy teacher and gave us all As and Bs. Because we all copied in Father Cristino's exams and Father Cristino, who knew, pretended he didn't notice and when he corrected the exams he would say from the platform, "How remarkable, what an excess of intelligence, what a capacity for abstract thought: I don't think any of you will fail in life . . ."

And I knew that Father Cristino was laughing at us with his As and Bs and I suspected that Father Cristino knew perfectly well who was going to fail in life, who life was going to pass and who was going to get a B. Because Father Cristino knew that life never gave us an A. It was the first thing Stein said to me. "Father Cristino is laughing at your friends." He said your friends as if he belonged to another caste, as if he wasn't even in the same class as us, or as if his grade in philosophy wasn't the same as ours, as if he'd just happened to be passing and said to me: they're laughing at your friends. But he didn't say they were laughing at me. And Stein's words remained engraved in my mind, especially when he said: Why don't you ask your parents for permission to come to my house next Sunday? And I didn't tell him that my parents weren't my parents but my grandparents, I said yes, I'd love to, and he said, I'll come and pick you up on Sunday afternoon, okay?

On Saturday nights, after having dinner, my grandfather would let me stay with them until eleven. Eleven was the time my grandparents went to bed and it was on Saturday nights that I talked to my parents, there in the smoking room, glued to the radio.

On top of the radio was a photograph of my parents in a brown leather frame. It had been taken three years earlier, not long after I had gone to live in my grandparents' house and my grandparents' house had become my own house. In the photograph my father was wearing a light-colored linen suit, a loosened tie, and a white shirt. He was looking at a map, with his head bent and his brow knitted. By his side stood my mother, wearing a flowered dress, glasses with white frames and a hat, and looking at my father as if looking at someone she knew, but couldn't quite place. In that photograph, taken in Singapore, it was very hot and there were some Chinese people in white shirts with blurred faces passing behind my parents. I barely recognized my parents in the photograph and I wondered who had been holding the camera, who had taken that photograph. My parents' faces were a succession of postcards of distant cities and that couple looking at a map in a street in Singapore seemed strange to me, as strange as the glass rooster next to my parents' photograph on the dark box-like radio; as strange as the sensation of my mother looking at my father on a street in Singapore.

The glass rooster was a barometer that changed color depending on the atmospheric pressure: mauve meant good weather and blue the threat of rain. That year the rooster was as blue as the sea in winter and we had to call the builders in on three occasions, because of leaks. I talked to my parents next to the rooster and the photograph in the brown leather frame. I would switch on the radio and between magnetic bleeps and noises that sounded like the rattle of machine guns I would turn the dial and go through the cities looking for my parents. In the centre of the dial was a metal circle: two stilletto-like needles radiated from it and went across the display screen crammed with names: Madrid, Oslo, Paris, Warsaw, Moscow, Budapest, Ankara, Saigon, Rabat, Peking, Vladivostok, Shanghai, Singapore . . . Yes, Singapore was part of that constellation of names, but my parents were in only one of those names and I knew it wasn't Singapore: too much time had passed since my grandparents' house had become my house. I would listen, between magnetic bleeps and the rattle of machine guns, to those voices in strange languages and I would think that perhaps, at that same moment, my parents were listening to those same voices and that without their knowing it, the three of us were all talking in the same strange language through the celestial chaos of the radio waves.

Then I would look at their photograph and the name of the city marked by the steel needle and the rooster, currently blue in color, and I would switch off the radio and the click of the radio as I switched it off was like the smack of lips on my hot cheek, so close was I to the radio, and those lips were those of my parents who were in one of the cities written there but not Singapore and they were kissing me because of the time that we had spent talking in a foreign language that Saturday night, like all Saturday nights, while my grandfather sat reading by the fire and my grandmother knitted a woolen sweater colored blue or grey or brown like a partridge's feathers or like my mother's eyes in the photograph taken by an invisible hand on a street in Singapore.

My grandfather didn't say no. My grandfather simply said: be careful of what you don't know and be home by eight, but he didn't say no. My grandmother, on the other hand, was silent, as she always was when my grandfather spoke and my grandmother's silence reflected my grandmother's attitude, which rejected lives that were not like hers, as if they didn't exist, she rejected them in silence, without speaking ill of anybody, but she rejected them with her silence. That, at least, was what I thought: that my grandmother's silence was her rejection of what she had always kept her distance from, but I was wrong, as men are when they don't know women.

That Sunday I hardly noticed the mass or the Sunday breakfast: chocolate instead of milk and sugar-coated pastries and cake instead of toast almost as black as the priests' cassocks on weekdays. I couldn't wait for the afternoon—and, with the afternoon, Guillermo Stein—to arrive. The only thing I noticed was that the hours were passing more slowly than usual and that my grandmother was quieter than usual and that my grandfather was paying more attention to my grandmother than usual. Nothing else, until the bell rang and the bell that rang was the little bell that Uncle Federico rang, not the electric bell the visitors rang, which had a sound like an insect trapped in a glass jar. And Guillermo Stein said hello to my grandfather respectfully, but not my grandmother, who had a headache and had retired to her room with a little bottle whose label read Distovagal, a little bottle my grandmother often took with her when she retired to her room at hours when she was normally never in her room. And my grandfather gave me three five-peseta bills so that we could take the bus, because Guillermo Stein's house was on the outskirts of the city, in a neighborhood called El Terreno, which I didn't know because my grandparents never took me for a walk farther than the limits of what had been the historic city walls. My grandparents always said that the only people who lived outside the walls were those who had something to hide.

"Here, treat your friend," my grandfather said, giving me three five-peseta bills so that we could take the bus. "Remember to be back home by eight."

And by eight I was back home, my head full of images of Guillermo Stein's neighborhood, Guillermo Stein's house, and Guillermo Stein's sister's smile; all these images paraded in front of me as if in a diorama, the kind my grandfather told me about when the time of the fair came and I fell ill with flu and he lent me his diorama and told me that he had always liked having dioramas. Because I always had flu when the fairground people came to the city and the flocks of swifts were like fireworks blackening the sky.

Guillermo Stein's house was a house filled with light: I had never seen so much light in a house. The Steins' neighborhood was a neighborhood of houses with gardens, a neighborhood that looked out onto the sea, and from the garden walls hung a blaze of bougainvillea, and jasmine and wisteria and ivy plunged to the street in green and white cataracts. The steep lanes of Guillermo Stein's neighborhood smelled better than the perfume shops my grandmother visited with me in tow, such was the profusion of scents on the steep lanes where the Steins lived. And the sidewalks were strewn with green and yellow petals and leaves, as if it were Corpus Christi, and that was because of the rain, although that afternoon it was only drizzling in the Steins' neighborhood, for the first time in many weeks it was only drizzling, a fine transparent rain that barely got you wet was falling and the rain was like an exercise in calligraphy on the pages of the sky.

The Steins' house did not have curtains and from all the windows you could see the sea. You went in through a tiled courtyard, a covered courtyard full of potted plants that led to a terrace with a glass canopy and to a garden. And from the courtyard, the terrace and the garden you could also see the sea; you could see the sea and the piers, the cranes like huge metal pelicans, the cargo boats and yachts at anchor. And in the background, the city, spread like a fan around the silvery bay, and in the middle of the city, the cathedral, like a fantastic ship of ocher stone, crowned by whimsical masts and arches and capstans, a galleon of gilded stone run aground on the walls. The bay and the city were part of the Steins' house; they came into the house the way the light of day and the darkness of night come into a house.

The furniture in the Steins' house was different than the furniture I was used to: the couches and armchairs were cube-shaped and upholstered in zebra skin or fabrics with geometric patterns: there wasn't much furniture considering how large the Steins' house was. And the other furniture was all of wood as smooth as jasper and round at the corners, with chromium-plated handles and metal inlays: the pieces of furniture looked like cars; they looked like Bugattis from the days when Fangio raced at Monte Carlo.

And the paintings were all brightly colored and there were bronzes of athletes and many portraits of men and women in a landscape or a tapestry or a mirror; I remember the portrait of a man carrying a macaw on his shoulder and his tie was the same color as the macaw's plumage; and the rugs also had geometric shapes, they were like metal sheets with geometric patterns in loud colors. I had never seen a house like the Steins' house, with so much light and so much sea and such outlandish furniture, furniture that, however outlandish it was, had a mysterious beauty, like an American film full of gangsters and hotels at night, or like the way Guillermo Stein looked at me as I was looking at Guillermo Stein's house.

Guillermo Stein lived with his father and sister. Guillermo Stein's sister's name was Paula, Paula Stein, and presumably his father didn't have a name because Stein didn't tell me what his father was called. All he said was, "My mother doesn't live with us; my mother abandoned my father soon after I was born." And then he said, "Let me show you my sister Paula's room and my father's study." And in his sister Paula's room the walls were lined with glass boxes and in the glass boxes there were hundreds of different butterflies, hundreds of butterflies in colors like the coats of arms in the atlas where the coat of arms on Guillermo Stein's bicycle did not appear. Paula Stein's collection was the first real collection I had ever seen in a house. It was more like a collection in a museum than a classmate's sister's collection. Because most of us in my class collected something: Califano, minerals; Fortuny, aviation prints; Prim, bullets and bullet cases; Jiménez, bottle tops; Forteza, movie posters; I collected postcards and cardboard soldiers; and Gual, American pin-up calendars that his father brought him from Hong Kong—it was said that his father had sold arms to Chiang Kai-shek from his office in Hong Kong. But none of us had a collection like Paula Stein's. None of us had a sister like Paula Stein.

I met Paula Stein twice in my life. The first time I fell in love with her. The second time I knew I would

47

never forget her. Stein and I were in his father's study the first time I met Paula Stein. The study was the one room in the house that had curtains, thick green velvet curtains, and familiar furniture: big, worn leather armchairs, a desk covered in papers, shelves piled high with boxes and files, and two lamps with canvas shades that filled the room with a light like raspberry jam. Because Guillermo Stein's father liked artificial light in his study and always kept the blinds down and the shutters closed, Guillermo Stein said. On the walls hung portraits of Central European aristocrats—they're Central European princes, Guillermo Stein told me—and I thought about the photograph taken on the day of Edward VII's funeral, because those photographs in Stein's father's study were also full of gaiters and decorations and silk sashes, but I didn't know any of those faces with big long mustaches and thick beards and uniforms with dolmans and gold braid. Even though I was consul of history I had never seen those faces looking down at Stein and me in Stein's father's study. It was then that Paula Stein appeared.

I was looking at one of Stein's father's cards, which read *Boris Negresco, attorney at law,* and at another, which read *Boris IV, King of Galicia.* Amazed by Stein's father's cards, I was just wondering if he was a forger pursued by various foreign police forces, and remembering what my grandparents had said about people living outside the walls because they had something to hide, when Paula Stein appeared in her father's study, smiling and completely naked.

I had never seen a naked woman before and, faced with Paula Stein's naked body, I didn't know what to do. Guillermo Stein seemed not to notice his sister's nudity, but as I stood there in the raspberry light of Stein's father's study, all I could see was Paula Stein's very white skin, Paula Stein's curly pubic hair, Paula Stein's dark nipples looking at me like two piercing eyes, while I made an effort to look at Paula Stein's smiling face, her eyes like honey-colored almonds, her pink lips, her teeth as white as her skin. Paula Stein smiled as she held out her hand to me and I was afraid I would brush against one of her breasts and at the same time I really wanted to brush against one of her breasts and I thought about Boris Negresco, attorney at law, and Boris IV, King of Galicia, as I shook Paula Stein's cold hand and Paula Stein's body was an alabaster lamp that had filled Stein's father's study with white light.

It was then that I became fully aware of something I had noticed on entering Stein's father's study: the smell of cats. Stein's father's study smelled mightily of cat's piss. But I'd happily have stayed forever in Stein's father's study, in spite of the cat smell, I'd have stayed there with Stein sitting in a worn leather armchair and Paula Stein, naked, smiling at me with her whole body. And Paula Stein was already turning her back on me, with her right hand on the handle of the door and her hair falling over one shoulder blade, leaving the back of her neck free, when I looked at the floor and saw her ankles, very slim ankles, and then I raised my eyes and saw her ass, the first ass I had ever seen in my life, the best ass I had ever seen in my life, and Stein laughed and I felt embarrassed that Stein was there, squatting in the armchair, looking at me as I looked at his sister's ass, and Paula Stein said, See you another day, and I was on the bus, on the way home, and thinking about that other day: that's why I took no notice of the old man with dyed hair and a thin mustache, wearing a jacket like a waiter's with whistles and colored ribbons hanging from it, who passed his tongue slowly over his upper lip, beneath his thin mustache, which was dyed black, a bluish black, and looked at me as he did so and laughed and finally stuck his tongue out at me, a pasty, violet tongue, and started singing in Italian, while I was thinking about Paula Stein and the Steins' house, and about how when we were in Stein's father's study it smelled of cat's piss—it smelled of cat and you could hear footsteps over Stein's father's study, as if someone was walking in the attic of the Steins' house.

That night I had a dream.

When I went to live in my grandparents' house, one of the Viala sisters gave me a holy book as a gift. "Now you have a holy book," Aunt Teresa Viala said when Aunt Rosa gave me the book, and I thought a holy book was a book with holes in it or something like that. And I laughed. Aunt Rosa got angry. She got angry with Aunt Teresa and she got angry with me. "The only things you're interested in are bridge, gin and men," Aunt Rosa said to Aunt Teresa, "please don't sneer at serious things, your laughter won't help you when the day of reckoning comes." I didn't know what bridge was, or gin, or the day of reckoning, or men—well, men, yes, though I didn't yet know what Aunt Rosa meant when she said "men," with a grimace of disgust on her lips, as if she had just eaten bitter fruit. And Aunt Teresa Viala laughed as I had laughed, and I laughed again and Aunt Rosa Viala said to me, "Read it, my dear, and you won't like feel like laughing then: you have to be prepared; a boy like you needs to be prepared." And Aunt Teresa Viala said, "Leave the boy alone, stupid." She said it affectionately, as if forgiving her for something and I assumed that what she was forgiving her for was the remark about bridge and gin and men. And the remark about bridge and gin and men, I thought, might be connected with what I had heard whispered: that a friend

51

of the family, the captain of a merchant ship, had blown his brains out because of Aunt Teresa.

That night too I had a dream and the dream set in motion, as if in my grandfather's diorama, a drawing from that book I had been given by Aunt Rosa Viala for when I stopped laughing. I had looked at that drawing for quite some time before going to sleep. That drawing fascinated me: it was a drawing of a bridge, a bridge so high it was more like an aqueduct; a bridge with ten arches, each one marked with a Roman numeral, from I to X, and each number was one of the Ten Commandments and at the end of the bridge there were some angels and over the bridge was the eye of God inside a triangle—"The All-Seeing Eye" according to the drawing—and under the bridge there was a mass of waves and flames and I wondered how it was possible for waves and flames to be together, and in among the waves and flames there were some scary monsters and below them some demons with tridents and tails who were urging on the scary monsters. And some people were crossing the bridge, going in the direction of the angels, and some were falling at arch number III and others at V and others at VI— many of them fell at VI—and more of them fell at IX, when they had almost gotten to the end, and some—very few—got to the end and those who got to the end had haloes over their heads as if

they were saints and those who fell into the jaws
of the monsters fell along with the stones from the
bridge because the bridge was crumbling at III,
V, VI or IX. And that night I dreamed about the
bridge. I dreamed I was going to fall from one of
those roman numerals, but I didn't know which
one, and so I kept very still before I got to the
first arch and the monsters were shrieking and it
was very hot and also very cold and I was still and
the bridge was crumbling, starting at the far end
and moving toward the beginning, where I was
very still, unable to turn and run away, and there
on arch number IV was the box with my postcards
and I saw the bridge crumbling and just as the
abyss opened up right before my feet I woke up.
I never dreamed again about that bridge until the
day I visited the Steins' house.

That night I dreamed again about the bridge
with the ten arches. Paula Stein stood at the end
of the bridge, naked, just as I had seen her in her
father's study. But it wasn't either cold or hot and
under the bridge there was only darkness. I could
hear footsteps behind me, footsteps behind my back
that sounded like the footsteps overhead in Stein's
father's study. And I saw Guillermo Stein coming
across the bridge towards me, chatting with the old
man from the bus, the old man who had licked his
blue mustache while looking at me and humming
in Italian. And the footsteps were getting louder

and louder and the bridge was shaking and I was starting to feel dizzy, but it was a sweet, gentle dizziness, and Paula Stein was running toward me to stop me falling, and Guillermo Stein and the old man with the dyed blue mustache were barring her way and I was falling, but it was neither cold nor hot, and suddenly I was in Paula Stein's arms and I felt a shaking that was even more intense than the shaking of the bridge, a shaking that took hold of me as I felt Paul Stein's flesh as if it were my flesh and then I woke up and noticed a hot, thick, damp patch in my pajama pants and I thought about the smell of cat's piss in the Steins' house, but the bed smelled not of cat's piss, but of bitter almonds, and I could still feel Paula Stein's flesh on my fingertips and I searched on my chest for the traces of Paula Stein's dark nipples.

2

Once a year, in spring, Uncle Federico came and picked me up in his car. Uncle Federico's car was a dark green Buick Roadster, and it was driven by Uncle Federico's chauffeur Francisco. The steering wheel of the Buick Roadster was made of wood, a very pale wood with black grain. Once a year, in spring, Uncle Federico's chauffeur drove me to Masvern, the farm where Uncle Federico lived with his father, that is, my great-grandfather, my grandfather's father. Francisco wore a chauffeur's uniform, a pearl-gray uniform with a cap and silver buttons. He ate lupin beans and blew his nose with his fingers. I always asked him why he blew his nose with his fingers and he always gave the same reply:

"You gentry are dirtier than us, you keep the muck in your pockets."

Uncle Federico's chauffeur would blow his nose with his fingers and fling the snot on the ground with an almost angry gesture, as if punishing the earth for making him a chauffeur, which I thought was unfair because lots of people would have liked to drive a car like Uncle Federico's Buick Roadster and wear a uniform as nice as Francisco's.

Masvern was a few kilometers from the city. I remember it as a very big house with lots of balconies and a central loggia with three arches that looked toward the almond field and an avenue lined with palm trees as tall and thin as the plumes of Bengal lancers. And dogs: there were lots of dogs at Masvern; big black dogs that scared me and leapt up and down and barked as we drove along the lane of palm trees and I never knew if they were barking because they were pleased to see Uncle Federico's Buick Roadster or if they were barking because they were angry and wanted to bite Francisco and me as soon as we got out of Uncle Federico's Buick Roadster.

And there at the door of the house was Uncle Federico, waiting for us with his Tuscan cigar between his teeth, and the dogs would fall silent and turn all docile when they saw Uncle Federico waiting there for us, holding a riding crop in his right hand and beating the right leg of his pants with it. And up above, in the loggia, was my great-grandfather. My great-grandfather was always in the loggia, dressed in a striped suit with a pair of binoculars slung around his neck. My great-grandfather's shoes were brown and looked like mirrors they were so clean, two cinnamon-colored mirrors full of bulges that smelled of cream, that always smelled of cream, not of shoe polish, but actual cream, that's how my great-grandfather's shoes smelled. And from time to time he would take the binoculars and look through them at the almond field and his face would light up—his grayish face would flush when it lit up—and he would cry, "I can see them, I can see them now; I can see them now in the yacht: there they are, the chorus girls from Berlin."

Then Uncle Federico would let out a laugh and, seeing that Uncle Federico was laughing, I would also laugh, but afterwards I didn't say anything because I never said anything at Masvern unless I was asked, except to ask Francisco, the chauffeur, why he blew his nose with his fingers when he had a handkerchief, and as for my being asked something, nobody ever asked me anything. And after lunch, Uncle Federico would retire to take his afternoon nap and I would go with my great-grandfather to the loggia, where he would sit down in his canvas rocking chair and wait; wait for the yacht with the chorus girls from Berlin to pass on a sea that was invisible because Masvern was built facing away from the sea. And I always felt very strange in Masvern; I didn't feel the way I felt in my grandparents' house or at school and the only thing I liked about Masvern was being with my great-grandfather while Uncle Federico had his siesta; sitting at the feet of my great-grandfather as he dozed in his chair and stroked my head like someone stroking the handle of a door and wondering whether or not to open it, because he suspects that if he opens it his life will never be the same again and, even though he's thoroughly bored with his life, the thought that it will never be the same again scares him.

And when Uncle Federico woke up from his nap, Francisco would park the car in front of Masvern and I would kiss my great-grandfather's forehead and run downstairs and there was Uncle Federico at the wheel with the engine already on, ready to drive me back to my grandparents' house, that is, to his sister's house, which he visited on Thursday evenings, taking advantage, he said, of the fact that he had to come to Palma to talk with his lawyer. And on the back seat of the Buick Roadster lay a basket with vegetables and a piece of sheep's-milk cheese, and when the car drew up outside the door of my grandparents' house, Uncle Federico would pick up the basket and say, "here, this is for your grandmother."

He always said for your grandmother, not for my sister or for my brother-in-law or for all of you, no: he said for your grandmother and I knew that the next morning my grandmother would take the basket with the vegetables and the sheep's-milk cheese to the Little Sisters of the Poor, because although my grandmother never said anything I knew that Masvern hid one of my grandmother's secret sorrows, the greatest of all after the absence of my parents. That was why I also never said anything at Masvern and felt like a stranger at Masvern, even though half my family had been born within its walls and seen their first daylight from the loggia, where my great-grandfather was now waiting for death, alone, looking through his binoculars at the chorus girls from Berlin.

When we left school, Jiménez, Planas and I would walk home together, because the three of us lived near each other. Going to war, we called it. That year, because of all the rain, the theatre of war was Indochina or Cambodia. The streets were like those of a city swept by monsoons and at any moment a cycle rickshaw might come around the corner with a thin-legged coolie pedaling under a straw hat that looked like a beach umbrella. We would walk very slowly, looking for victims. We were looking for people walking on the streets who seemed suspicious and we would make up stories about them, invent a shady past that was the reason for their walking in that suspicious way.

"That one is definitely a German war criminal," Jiménez said under his breath.

And we hid in the doorway, waiting for our war criminal to pass, a man in a green hat and a double-breasted trench coat who had to be German precisely because he was wearing a green hat and a double-breasted gabardine coat and who had to be a war criminal precisely because he was German, and then we followed him to see if he left any clues behind him that would confirm our suspicions. And the German went into a shoeshine parlor and the glass front of the shoeshine parlor was black and as we waited we pretended cycling on the black glass, which divided us down the middle, reflecting our images formed of two identical halves, two identical halves pedaling in the void and laughing at our own caricatures, laughing at the symmetrical magic of the black glass of the shoeshine parlor.

"That one must be a Soviet agent on a secret mission," Planas said.

So we abandoned our German war criminal in the shoeshine parlor and pursued our Soviet agent, who had close-cropped hair like in Erich von Stroheim movies, and was walking in silence to a clandestine appointment in some waterfront dive. An appointment with members of the resistance: Communists, Republicans and a foreign woman, one of those foreign women who smoked through a mother-of-pearl cigarette holder and wore butterfly-shaped glasses—a femme fatale's glasses, Jiménez said—one of those foreign women who could only be spies of some enemy power, sitting there in a waterfront tavern with two or three nasty-looking men who were laughing the way we laughed in the black glass front of the shoeshine parlor, laughing a lot so that nobody would know that they were in the pay of Soviet intelligence. And our gray raincoats were camouflage jackets: we were gray shadows that the rain slid off as we walked on the gray rain-drenched streets of a city that could have been Macao or Saigon. And Planas's eyes lit up, like an animal lying in wait, and he said, "Let's go see the old man with the Messerschmitt."

And we set off at a run down the hill to the sewing machine repair shop whose owner had a car that was actually the cockpit of a Messerschmitt and just then he was lowering the metal shutter of his repair shop, a shutter as gray as the railings around a cemetery, where he only repaired old sewing machines and then he got into his car, the cockpit of a Luftwaffe bomber on the sheet metal of which there were some big white numbers and lots of rivets and the black cross of the German army, which had been scratched out with sandpaper but was still visible as the black cross of the German army. And the car had only three wheels and one silver headlamp that looked dirty in the rain falling on the city. And Planas said, "When I'm older I'm going to buy Señor Martínez's car." Because on the shutter there was a blue and red painted sign with green lettering that said: *Diego Martínez. Sewing machines repairing*, as if the machines fixed themselves.

And Jiménez was the first to get home and then Planas and I was the last one to get home and first would walk through the area with the movie theaters and read their names: the Rivoli, the New Orleans, the Rialto, the Luxor, the Excelsior, the Trocadero, the Beverly, the Positano, and the names of the movie theaters and the colorful photographs in their display cases and the titles of the movies carried back to me the faces of my parents, the faces enclosed in the cardboard box that I kept in my room at number twelve Via Portugal.

On those expeditions, the Steins seemed to me like characters in a dream, characters in a distant dream that could barely be remembered.

"Sit down, Miralles, come on, will you, sit down, you're not going to start crying right here, are you, in front of your classmates?"

Miralles sat down, looking very pale. He sat down with reddened eyes, Miralles did, on the verge of tears; Miralles's hands were trembling and he was biting his tongue not to cry after the Father Prefect had just read out his grades: a disaster, Miralles, a magnificent harvest of failing grades, Miralles, I don't know what you're thinking of doing with your life, but this is shameful, I'll have to speak to your parents.

"There are some of you who bring shame to the school," continued the Father Prefect, looking us in the eyes one by one, stressing each word as if dropping stones. "Young Turks, that's what you are, young Turks straight from the ranks of Ataturk, dunces intent on destroying our civilization."

The Father Prefect's name was Riudavets, and he could as easily have been the commandant of a prison camp or a subaltern in the Foreign Legion as a Father Prefect. Father Riudavets was our enemy—whether we had good or bad marks, whether we were excellent pupils or terrible pupils, Father Riudavets was our enemy. He knew it, and he liked it. He liked being our enemy.

"I want supermen, my friends, not the dregs of humanity. Next year, when you study Nietzsche, you'll understand. Now let's see, Montaner . . ."

And Montaner stood up, also looking very pale, even though he knew he was going to get good grades; Montaner knew that that month he was getting mostly *excellent* or at the very least *honorable mention* in the report, indicated by laurel leaves, and if things went well, even *distinction*, with a neo-classical border. But Montaner stood up from his chair as if he were going to be failed in everything and pretended to look Father Riudavets in the eyes, which was what Father Riudavets demanded, but Montaner was actually looking a little higher; Montaner was looking at the blackboard, as we all

63

did when we heard our names called: we looked at the blackboard but pretended to be looking Father Riudavets in the eyes.

Those of us who had good grades Father Riudavets dispatched in a few minutes—"Ridorsa, top honors; Planas, top honors"—with a blank look on his face as if in a particularly unpleasant trance, but when, in that book with its sinister metal covers, he caught sight of a wounded animal he could get his teeth into and not let go, the corners of Father Riudavets's lips went up and we all saw his white fanglike canines glittering beneath Father Riudavets's pasty skin.

"Now, let's see, Salom, stand up. Stand up, man, what a stupendous year you're having. What months you've been having, Salom, let's see if this month we outdo ourselves."

And as he turned the page, his skin became pastier and his teeth glittered more brightly and then he whispered in a gravelly voice:

"Of course we outdid ourselves, how could we not outdo ourselves? Salom, you're a phenomenon. Let's see: religion, a four, an almighty four ... Salom, Salom ... Where are you from, Salom? From the ranks of Ataturk or the hordes of Attila? You're a human disaster, Salom, a sick quadruped, Salom, getting only a four in religion ... Why not a two, Salom, or a one, why not just a one? It's less of a figure, it takes less effort. I suppose that's the first four in your life. Your days are numbered in this school, Salom: you're a walking disgrace."

That was how Father Riudavets put it: your days are numbered, Salom, and Salom actually did cry, Salom burst into tears over his desk, covering his nose and mouth with his hands, and Father Riudavets said, "Would you like a handkerchief, Señor Salom? Or should I call you Señorita?"

And after Salom came Stein.

"Top honors, Stein. Congratulations."

And Stein heard top honors like someone hearing rain, with his eyes fixed on the window where the rain disfigured the trees in the courtyard and a cold smile on his face, a smile that almost imperceptibly shook the hieratic Father Riudavets, as if Stein knew that behind Father Riudavets's icy exterior lay a clay puppet, so pasty was his face. And Stein looked at the rain and smiled, and Father Riudavets said, "Sit down, Stein," and the echo of that "Sit down, Stein" sounded between the white walls of the classroom like "I'll get you one of these days, Stein: we still have time. We both have plenty of time ahead of us."

My grandfather didn't care about grades. My grandfather considered it the most natural thing in the world that I should get good grades. But he took advantage of the day when I brought my report book home to talk to me about other things. My grandfather would sit at the desk in his study, beneath his collection of sabers, pistols and Moroccan daggers, and while waiting for me he would tidy the desk drawers, or pretend to tidy the drawers, which were impossible to tidy because they were already tidier than the tins of tobacco in a cigar store. And from the drawers he would take out a mechanical tortoiseshell fan, a little hand fan that my grandfather used in summer, a pocket watch, and some photographs from the Africa campaign, photographs from when he had fought in Africa and had defended a position for five months, the besieged fort of Tizzi-Asa against Abd el-Krim's Riffian troops. My grandfather always took out the same things and I knew, when he sat waiting at the desk in his study and took out the hand fan, the gold watch and the photographs of Morocco, that my grandfather wanted to tell me something, even though he pretended to be tidying his drawers, and didn't care about the number of times *excellent* or *outstanding* had been written in black ink in the stamped pages of my blue report book.

"Your grandmother doesn't like you going to the Steins' house. It's all the same to me, everything that is supposed to happen in this life ends up happening. And besides, I trust you: you've never disappointed me. But the Steins aren't like us, your grandmother says. In fact, your grandmother says they are the exact opposite of us and you know your grandmother is always right."

I didn't understand a word of what my grandfather was saying. I even started thinking, as I sat there beside the glass-fronted bookcase in my grandfather's study, that my grandfather was speaking in mysterious hieroglyphics, in some language that could only be understood once I had cracked the code. And that my grandfather knew it, that my grandfather was doing it on purpose to test his grandson's intelligence, above and beyond the numbers written in the blue report book. But I also thought about the word Stein in the smoking room of our house as we had dinner, and how Stein had seemed to me a word as sinister as the hissing of a cobra, not because I thought Stein's surname was a sinister word, no, but because my grandfather thought of Stein as sinister and dangerous and had communicated that thought to me through those invisible threads by which people in the same family always end up thinking the same.

"There's a postcard from your parents," my grandfather said, closing the drawers of his desk. "It's on the mantelshelf in the dining room."

I ran to get it. It was a view of Buenos Aires taken from an airplane—that was what it said on the back: *View of Buenos Aires taken from an airplane*—but I didn't read any more; I didn't read the words my mother had written in her angular handwriting in the bar of some hotel in Buenos Aires. And I added the city of Buenos Aires to my images of my parents. As if adding a wrinkle to my parents' faces. For the first time in my life, as if I were adding a wrinkle to them.

"The Congress of Vienna. Today we're going to talk about the Congress of Vienna, the funeral of Napoleonic Europe—a funeral of dubious, indeed even perverse morality, though led by an admirable man, Chancellor Metternich. Now, Ridorsa, tell your classmates about the crafty schemes of that Frenchie rascal Prince Talleyrand, and the chancellor's strategy to counter his underhand schemes . . ."

I was the secretary to Father Ribas, our history teacher. As the consul of history it fell to me to be Father Ribas's secretary. Because Father Ribas needed a secretary. "This school ought even to give me a butler," he would say. And I, as the secretary, would give my classmates their grades, grades that Father Ribas would mutter in a guttural voice, using a complicated system based on naval battles. He explained all about it on the first day of class.

"Gentlemen"—Father Ribas always called us gentlemen—"I like naval battles. And you, being in my charge, have no choice but to like naval battles. During the year each of you will have a fleet: two galleons, four schooners and five sloops.

The day I sink your fleet, and I will sink them little by little if you don't answer my questions correctly, you will be doomed. Doomed, do you hear me? You will go straight to the catacombs: to the ca-ta-combs. R.I.P., you'll be dead and the fish will eat your eyes out. But if you study from now until September, you may come back to life and cry land ahoy."

I kept my fleet intact, but I was one of the few. Father Ribas was like a submarine commander, causing more havoc in the Atlantic than the iceberg that sank the Titanic.

"Sink that numbskull Prim's last remaining sloop, sink it. A name like yours, Prim, and you don't know anything about Amadeo of Savoy . . . How do you spend your time? Fishing? Well, now you're going to see the fish up close. You'll see how cute those little fish are up close, with their little scales and their stupid little mouths. I'm not sure who they remind me of, Prim, with their stupid little mouths."

And I sank the last sloop remaining in Prim's fleet. I sank it and I didn't enjoy sinking it but nor did I suffer in the slightest. The rules of the naval battle were the same for everybody and in Father Ribas's notes, Amadeo of Savoy was taken care of in three lines, so it wasn't difficult. Not for Prim, not for anybody. Modern Spanish history wasn't difficult for anybody, because Father Ribas didn't like modern Spanish history, and so he skipped over it—five lines for the Carlist wars, seven for the War of Independence—as if tiptoeing through something shameful.

"If at least Spain and Portugal had united," Father Ribas would say, "but the way things went, from the eighteenth century onwards everything was a disaster, believe me. What a big mistake Philip II made in not moving the capital to Lisbon . . ."

The afternoon we tackled the Congress of Vienna, Father Ribas was very nervous. He kept looking up at the ceiling and moving his right hand over his glasses. He was moving his hand over his glasses as if there were a spiderweb in front of his glasses. I was talking about the role of Metternich's secret police at the congress when Father Ribas interrupted me.

"Stop, Ridorsa, stop! Can't you see the cracks in the ceiling?"

I looked up: there were no cracks in the ceiling. I put on a blank look.

"What, Ridorsa? Can't you see the cracks threatening us? You need to go to an optician, my friend. What about the others: can't you see the cracks in the ceiling? That ceiling is going to come crashing down on us. We have to change classrooms immediately."

Father Ribas stood there as if hypnotized, looking up at the ceiling.

"This is sabotage," he cried suddenly, kicking the platform, "sa-bo-tage. And I know who did it. Riudavets—the anarchist is Riudavets."

We started moving the book, the exercise books and the pens, looking at each other in astonishment; we didn't know what to do while the name of the Father Prefect echoed beneath the cracked ceiling of Father Ribas, seized with his own sudden madness.

"No, he doesn't know what to do to bring me down, that scoundrel Riudavets. He's never tolerated aristocrats of the spirit like me. He wants to liquidate us one by one, the damned Jacobin. Although that won't be too hard for him in this community of plebs: I'm the only one who'll stand up to him. But stand up to him I will. Ridorsa, call the fire department."

And as he told me to call the fire department, Father Ribas stooped and went under the desk. Once hidden under the desk, he started reciting the *Confiteor Deo*.

Stein stood up from his desk and went to Fortuny. He said something in his ear. Stein whispered some words in Fortuny's ear as if Stein were Palou, as if Stein were our captain, not the Guillermo Stein who had arrived in the middle of the year. And Stein's gesture did not escape Palou's notice, although Palou acted as if it had escaped his notice. Fortuny, who was the representative of our class, stood up and left the room. A few minutes later, he returned with the Father Prefect and Father Laval. When Father Ribas heard Riudavets's voice, he got up from under the table, yelling, "You're going to pay for this, Riudavets. This very afternoon I'm going to phone the Father General. And it'll go all the way up to the Vatican, Riudavets, yes, the Vatican. You're done for, Riudavets, you third-rate Robespierre. If I hadn't realized, you'd have spoiled the lives of my boys."

We never saw Father Ribas again, and none of us ever again talked about Father Ribas's sudden delirium. Not even Prim, whom he had persecuted and whose fleet he had sunk. We all liked Father Ribas a lot, he was the one teacher who called us gentlemen and liked naval battles. In the mornings, at mass, we would look for him in the choir stalls; we would look toward the choir to see if we could see Father Ribas among the hands and waxen faces of those who sat in the choir stalls waiting for their death. But we never saw him again: instead, Father Riudavets walked up and down the choir stalls, making a note of those who talked during the mass.

That year we all passed in Father Ribas's course; even Prim, who had no ships left. Nobody failed in Father Ribas's course, we all called him Hirohito and I still don't know why we called him Hirohito, because Father Ribas didn't look like the Emperor

Hirohito. But when he vanished from the school, we never again called him Hirohito.

The day Father Ribas lost his mind, we saw Stein's father. It was Planas, on the way out of school, who told us. As if firing a gun. His words were like a sharp gunshot in the rain.

"That's Stein's father."

"How do you know it's Stein's father?"

"I just know, believe me," Planas replied. "I'll explain."

The three of us waited for Stein's father to finish smoking his cigarette outside the school chapel. Stein's father was wearing a black leather trench coat and mountaineer's boots, brown boots with military soles and buckles, the boots I had heard overhead when I was in his study. He was big and strong, very tall, but the features of his face were the most difficult features to retain that I've ever seen in my life. Even today I wouldn't be able to describe the features of Stein's father's face, or the color of his eyes, or whether he had a mustache or not, or whether he had a mustache that didn't look like a mustache. Planas homed in on the same thing as me.

"He's the man with the invisible face," said Planas.

When Stein came out of school, he walked in his direction, but made as if he hadn't seen him. He took the chain off the back wheel of his bicycle and put it in his pigskin case, the case that had a stain like the map of Africa and that looked like a teacher's briefcase and not a pupil's satchel. Then, just as Stein was about to get on his bicycle, Stein's father grabbed Stein by the shoulder. He almost fell, Stein did, when his father grabbed him by the shoulder. They exchanged a few words and Stein looked troubled, as if he was ashamed at the thought that someone might see him on the street talking to his father.

"What if it isn't his father?" Jiménez said. "It could be a stranger threatening Stein."

"It's his father, Jiménez," replied Planas. "I tell you it's his father. I know, I saw his photograph among my Uncle Raimundo's papers."

And Stein set off on his bicycle, beneath his red rain cape, and the man that Planas said was Stein's father came striding in our direction. He passed us, Stein's father did, without seeing us, without even so much as a sidelong glance at us. We followed him. But this pursuit wasn't like the others, it wasn't like the ones where we invented a story for the object of our pursuit, in this case we were hoping that the object of our pursuit would give us a clue to his own history. And I was thinking about Boris Negresco, attorney at law; about Boris IV, king of Galicia; about Planas's words: "I saw his photograph among my Uncle Raimundo's papers," because

74

those words were a sign that Planas was already compiling his report on Stein.

Stein's father stopped after five blocks, outside a watchmaker's shop, and went inside. It was a watchmaker's shop that we knew because it was always empty and in the window it had an extraordinary collection of antique pocket watches, watches with faces of many colors, old enameled faces that stood out against the velvet background like a miniature Pacific atoll, a luminous archipelago lost in the middle of the ocean. We really liked the window of the Osiris watchmaker's shop. But we liked its owner even more, a bad-tempered man who always yelled at us and shooed us away from the window. He would come out onto the street in his shirtsleeves, with a tubular device in his left eye, a Bakelite tube with a lens that made his left eye look bigger, and two metal armbands on his forearms that held his sleeves in place, and would shoo us away, yelling, "Go to your homes, you Berbers, go to your parents and leave me alone, I'm sick and tired of you." And he would yell the word "Berbers" in a solemn tone, as if singing opera in a trembling voice inside an underground cave.

The afternoon Father Ribas went crazy the watchmaker didn't yell. He was very pale as he listened to Stein's father, who was waving some papers with wax seals and blue ribbons in front of the watchmaker's cyclopean glass eye. When Stein's father entered the shop, the watchmaker drew the curtains across the window, yellowing net curtains hanging from a grimy brass rail, but the light inside the shop allowed us to see the scene clearly.

"He has a gun!" Jiménez cried. "Stein's father has a gun!"

And Planas and I also saw the gun. A silver-plated pistol with mother-of-pearl inlays on the grip. We only saw it for a few seconds, because someone suddenly switched out the light and when the light went out we ran off. We ran off as if Stein's father were threatening us with his gun.

We didn't see Stein's father again. Until his photograph appeared in the newspapers, we didn't see Stein's father again.

This is what Planas told us:

"I haven't been able to find out where Stein is from, but what I have found out is that this isn't the first time Stein's father has lived in this city. He was here before, during the war. Stein's father isn't called Stein, but Piglia; his name is Fortunio Piglia and he was born in Palermo, Sicily. It's true that he knew Count Ciano, just as Stein said. He knew Count Ciano and my Uncle Raimundo during the war. Stein's father came to the island during the war: he came with the Italian pilots who bombed

76

Barcelona. But he never bombed Barcelona, or piloted a plane." Planas didn't say plane, he said Savoia Marchetti, because Planas knew everything there was to know about World War II and it was the same planes, Planas said, that bombed Barcelona and flew in World War II.

"He never piloted a plane because he belonged to Mussolini's secret service. The service that operated outside the country and was under the control of Count Ciano. They eliminated political opponents exiled in foreign cities and considered possible acts of war in neighboring countries. Ours, for example. Stein's father was one of the brains that planned to make the island Italian and convert it into a province of Fascist Rome. That was why he came dressed as an Italian pilot, with his big white scarf and his black leather jacket, which is how he appears in the photograph I found among my Uncle Raimundo's papers. But then things got complicated: someone who worked at the Italian consulate died, or something like that, I couldn't find out exactly what, and Stein's father disappeared. He hid in my Uncle Raimundo's house: Fortunio Piglia and my Uncle Raimundo had become great friends. Uncle Raimundo's brother, Murat, who you know, told me about it."

Planas looked at Jiménez and me. We did indeed know Murat because he talked to Murat on the street and had an enormous mustache, "a mustache like a Napoleonic hussar," Jiménez had said the first time we saw him. And what's more, he brandished his walking stick as if it were a saber. Planas' uncle was called Joaquín, but we called him Murat. He was a surgeon, he wore a bow tie, and he talked to himself on the street: he talked to himself, reciting Napoleon's battles: Jena, Austerlitz, Marengo . . . and when he got to Waterloo he would lower his walking stick and stop pensively in the middle of the street. What a calamity, my dear Murat, what a calamity! he would say in a low voice. That was why we called him Murat and followed him along the street. We liked following him along the street, even though Planas didn't like it as much as we did and would soon point out another target: "That one must be a Soviet agent," Planas would say, and we would leave Murat looking dejected in the middle of the street, as if the street were the hills of Waterloo.

"My Uncle Raimundo and Stein's father went to the front together," Planas continued. "They were both at the Battle of the Ebro, in water up to their waists for weeks, unable to move from their position. When the war was over Uncle Raimundo came back alone, without Stein's father. There was some kind of an attempt to buy some plantations in the Philippines, but I wasn't able to get the details. I was told about that by Murat, but Murat is a bit confused when he tells anecdotes about his brother. Uncle Raimundo wrote everything down in a series of diaries from the army geographical service. All this I found in one of his diaries. In one where the handwriting is like a trail of ants: it was quite an effort to understand it. But that's all I know."

"What about his mother, what do you know about Stein's mother?" Palou asked.

"I don't know anything about his mother," Planas said, smiling. "You know I know nothing at all about women."

This is what Planas told us, after Palou, in the courtyard, had said, "Out with it, Planas, you've made us wait long enough. What do you know about Stein's father?"

And when Planas stopped speaking, the sky was like a black umbrella, a black umbrella that someone had riddled with bullets.

This is what Palou replied:

"You disappoint me, Planas. I wasn't expecting such rubbish from you. You know that isn't the whole story about Stein's father. You know there's more: much more. And all the things you're hiding have a lot to do with one of us. With Ridorsa, for example. And also with you."

Palou looked at me. He looked at me as if to say: wait and see, you're such a friend of Planas, you are, such a friend of Planas and now you're going to find out about Planas.

"It's true about Stein's father, it's true about Count Ciano and his stupid bellic operetta plans and disembarking on the island and all that nonsense. But there's more. You haven't told us how Ridorsa's father, who also worked in the Italian consulate, discovered that Stein's father, in other words Fortunio Piglia, and your uncle had been the thugs who had bumped off the secretary of the consulate, a suspicious fellow, that secretary, and your uncle and Stein's father went too far, a murky business, something to do with illegal gambling dens, I don't know exactly, and afterwards they accused Ridorsa's father, Don Paolo, of the death. They reported your father to the police, Ridorsa, in those days it was very easy to get someone arrested and your father ended up in prison. But your Uncle Federico was able to intervene and arrange things and get him out of prison—by paying, of course. Your uncle Federico had a certain amount of influence over the authorities in the new regime. But even so it cost a lot of money: it cost your grandmother her inheritance, which all went on buying arms, I suppose, the war and all that. Which can't have bothered your uncle Federico too much, because it meant his getting his hands on the farm at Masvern and enjoying even more influence. The matter of your father was fixed and he was able to get back to normal, but things weren't the way they had been before. They had been living in Madrid

for a few years when the war ended, they had a
business importing Argentinian products, I believe.
And just before you were born they came back.
They'd made a lot of money and they thought this
money would protect them from disgrace. Your
mother tried to live here again, but she didn't last
more than ten years. She couldn't bear it. After ten
years she left. She left because she couldn't bear
the looks people gave her on the street, or the
comments they made; she couldn't bear the fact
that she wasn't invited to parties, when she had
been the life and soul of every party before the war;
she couldn't bear everybody avoiding her when
she went visiting because they still thought your
father, Ridorsa, was a criminal. The idea that your
father, who wasn't a criminal, could be a criminal,
was something your mother really couldn't bear. Or
the fact that you would have to pay the price too,
when you grew up. And in the meantime, Planas,
your Uncle Raimundo was cool as a cucumber.
Nobody believed that your Uncle Raimundo, who
came from such a good family—a bit dissolute, yes,
but who wasn't at that time?—could have been so
shameless as to accuse an innocent man. No: it had
to be Paolo Ridorsa, who was a foreigner and had
committed the sin of marrying one of the most
beautiful women in the city: your mother, Ridorsa.
It had to be Paolo Ridorsa. Why else would he
have come here, why didn't he live in Italy? And

when your uncle died, Planas, nothing happened: a few lines in the newspaper and his souvenirs of the Russian campaign. When you're somebody, it's easy to to fake your own life and your own death, if necesssary. That's something my father, who's very accustomed to dealing with corpses, always told me. But I'll tell you, Planas, I'll tell you some day what your uncle died of—or rather, why your uncle was killed, a man who'd been a hero of the Russian campaign and ended up a common black marketeer dealing in contraband medicines. I'll tell you one of these days.

"As for Stein, our silent friend Stein doesn't have a mother because his father gambled her away, two years ago. Can you imagine that? As if she were a boat or a house: he gambled her away. It was in a casino in France and he lost her to an Arab sheik, one of those oil-rich sheiks you see all over the world now loaded with dollars. That was why she abandoned Stein's father and the children of Stein's father. If you look in Stein's desk, you'll find a photograph of his mother. It's in one of his red exercise books. She was also very beautiful, Stein's mother was. Almost as beautiful as yours, Ridorsa."

And then Palou stopped speaking. At last Palou stopped speaking. None of us had said a word while Palou had been speaking. We all knew Palou didn't lie. Palou was the nephew of a canon of the Curia and the son of a chief inspector of the secret police, the B.I.S., and when he told us something, we all knew that he was telling us the truth. That was why I rushed at Palou, our consul of mathematics. For the first time in my life I felt the urge to kill. I wanted to kill Palou. And Palou hit me in the face, making me fall to the floor. And when I saw Palou coming toward me, saying, "I told you people like Stein upset the balance," I was afraid. And I didn't know if I was afraid of Palou, of what Palou had told us, or if I was afraid because I'd felt the urge to kill, but what I did know is that I would always be afraid and I thought about my parents, I don't know why, I thought about my parents and it struck me that they had never been by my side, that I had never known my parents and that was why I was afraid, that was why I would always be afraid. Just then, the whistle blew.

Father Laval was blowing his chromium-plated whistle to announce the end of recess.

The following morning Uncle Federico came for me in his dark green Buick Roadster. Francisco wasn't driving: Uncle Federico was driving and the car stank of cigar smoke. He took the highway in the direction of Masvern. He barely said anything during the ride: that this year the grapes and figs were going to be a disaster, with all this rain; that the almond harvest would go to waste; that his dog Estrella had had four puppies; and that Francisco was ruining the gear changes. "He drives her too hard," he said, "that lout will end up destroying my car." But apart from that, he only opened his mouth to blow out the smoke from his cigar.

I watched the movement of the windshield wipers and tried to synchronize it with the plane trees that lined the road. The rain formed an iridescent film over the glass, a film like my grandmother's eyes the previous night, when I had come home from school and, while we were having dinner in the smoking room, had told them part of what I had heard in the courtyard of the school. Only part, because I didn't dare tell all of it. I didn't dare and I couldn't. My grandfather said nothing, but my grandmother, her eyes like the iridescent film over the windshield wipers, got up from the table and said to my grandfather, "This has to stop once and for all. I'm going to call Federico."

And when I had finished dinner I went straight to bed. I went to bed with a burden of guilt, guilt at having crossed a threshold that should not have been crossed, and I took the box where I kept my parents' postcards and looked at those streets I knew by heart, those streets that knew my parents better than I did. Until I fell asleep. I don't know how long I had been asleep when I saw my grandfather come into the room, remove the postcards from the bedspread, switch off the night light, and then sit looking at me from the other bed, looking at me while I lay there half-asleep, thinking about Paula Stein.

The following morning, Uncle Federico came for me in his dark green Buick Roadster.

When we reached Masvern, he went into his study, a large room just to the right of the entrance, and came out carrying two shotguns.

"Today you and I are going hunting," he said, giving me the smaller of the two, a shotgun with very narrow barrels and a very shiny butt, a butt so small it was like the butt of an espingarda shotgun. "Sixteen millimeters, son," Uncle Federico said. "Not a single wood pigeon will be able to resist you."

We started walking. He lit a cigar and we started walking in silence. We walked for two hours without saying a word to each other. We both knew we weren't going hunting: with all the rain, not even the leaves would be flying today. After two hours we took shelter in a little shed beneath the oak trees. Uncle Federico lit another cigar, left the shotgun on the ground and started speaking. It was the only time in my life that I heard Uncle Federico string together more than three sentences in a row.

"Son, the world of adults is a pigsty. Why do you think I'm living here, without seeing anybody except my father—which means without seeing anybody, because my father is a vegetable with eyes, binoculars and chorus girls from Berlin, but a vegetable all the same? Because the world of adults is a pigsty. Why do you think your parents travel from city to city, never stopping in any one place for more than three months? Because the world of adults is a pigsty. If you aren't dirty, the world of adults will dirty you; if you aren't dirty enough, it'll try to dirty you a little more. That is the adult world and everything else is nonsense, believe me. You live in the best of worlds: on one hand, you have school, where there are no adults, because I've never yet met a priest who was an adult—how can they be, living cut off from women, and surrounded by boys all day long? It's impossible—and on the other hand, you have your grandparents, who are old, and for that very reason they aren't adults anymore. And besides, they love you, and you know something? It isn't easy for adults to love each other. Everyone acts out of self-interest, you scratch my back, I'll scratch yours, let's see what I can get out of that idiot, and it goes on and on, each day another blow, or even two. Everyone acts out of self-interest, envy and vanity: anything else is either a fool's game or a complete waste of time. And let's not even talk about when times get rough. You're not alone, kid—don't think you're alone, that would be a mistake. And besides, you're intelligent. But it's up to you, and only you, to make sure the world of adults doesn't drag you down. It'll always be up to you, your whole life long. Forget what you've been told and let the rest of us sort out the mess. And now shoot, shoot in the air, at the trees, wherever you like. Hold and shoot, boy, it'll relieve you—you don't know what a relief it is to shoot."

And Uncle Federico opened his pouch and passed me a handful of cartridges.

I started shooting. I shot and shot until I lost count of the number of shots and little by little the smell of powder stirred me until I started crying. Until I threw the shotgun on the ground and started crying as I had never cried before, hugging my Uncle Federico. We stood there hugging in the rain, under the oaks, both knowing that it was impossible to forget everything I had heard.

It was only a few weeks to the end of the school year when the rain finally abated. From time to time, there would be a cloudburst, then it would clear up, and after a few hours there would be another cloudburst, but it was definitely raining much less. The city filled with birds. I mean the birds flew, chirruped in the eaves of the buildings, and sang in the trees; it stopped being a city without birds; for the first time in many months it was again a city with both birds and sun. There were pupils who started coming to school by bicycle. Along the narrow cobbled street that led to the gates of the school you could again hear the tinkle of bells, the brakes like muffled sirens in the harbor, the spluttering sound of the chains when reversing. We talked louder on the street, we talked on the street as if we were acting in an open-air theater. And Stein suddenly stopped coming to school.

Nobody asked after him. Since the day I had fought with Palou, we had barely looked at Stein. And none of us knew if the reason we didn't look at Stein was because Stein had turned into a leper, or because we felt ashamed of ourselves when we looked at Stein, because we were the ones who felt like lepers because of what had happened and we avoided looking at Stein, in order not to infect him. None of us knew. And he acted as if he hadn't even noticed our attitude: he continued smiling with the same smile he had had on the first day, when he came to school by bicycle halfway through the year, a year when none of us came to school by bicycle.

The day Stein stopped coming to school, Jiménez brought in a newspaper and left it on my desk. It was very strange seeing a newspaper in class. None of us ever carried money in our pockets, let alone enough to buy a newspaper, something that was in every house anyway, and something you read at home, not at school.

"Page 12, Ridorsa, read page 12: the crime reports," Jiménez said in a low voice.

I opened the newspaper at page 12. And there on page 12, staring up at me, was a blurred photograph of Stein's father; the indistinct features of Stein's father's face made that blurred photograph seem even more blurred. I read the headline: INTERNATIONAL FORGER ARRESTED. "The arrest has been made in our city of the Italian Fortunio Piglia, alias Boris Negresco, who also passed himself off as King Boris IV of Galicia, a province of the former Austro-Hungarian Empire, today part of the Communist Republic of Poland. The felon, who was detained along with his partner in crime, the Spaniard B.B.F., a watchmaker by profession, forged noble titles from those crowns now exiled in Madrid because of the establishment in their countries of the cruel, atheistic Communist system. Having been informed, the private secretaries of King Leka of Albania, the Tsar of Bulgaria, the King of Montenegro and the King of Romania—all now resident in Madrid under the protection of His Excellency Generalísimo Francisco Franco Bahamonde, who has added the charm of a cosmopolitan court to the traditions of the capital—are trying to ascertain the number of false titles issued by the aforementioned Fortunio Piglia. These noble titles were apparently much prized among those who have made their fortunes in the past few years trading on the black market. The prisoner is now waiting for the Undersecretary of the Interior to decree, through the Civil Governor of the Province, his expulsion from Spanish soil, an expulsion which, according to reliable sources, appears imminent. The police are continuing their investigations to unearth other possible accomplices in this criminal plot."

When I finished reading the news of Stein's father's arrest, Palou was looking at me from his desk and in Palou's eyes, for a few seconds, I saw the same look my Uncle Federico had had amid the oaks at Masvern, in the rain, when he had said: let the rest of us sort out the mess.

That afternoon I slipped out of school. It was the first and only time I slipped out of school, in order to go to the Steins' house.

The Steins' neighborhood smelled of damp earth. The gardens in Stein's neighborhood were a jungle contained by walls, a jungle that smelled of damp earth and the scent of jasmine and morning glory. The doors of the Steins' house were wide open. The sea was a raft of blue paint streaked with orange juice. A cargo boat with a red and black hull was entering the harbor. There were a lot of packages in the tiled courtyard of the Stein's house.

You couldn't see the plant pots, or the well, or the white brick benches with their yellow stars. All you could see in the Steins' courtyard were packages. I went into the house.

Guillermo Stein was on the terrace beyond the living room, looking at the city, the houses, laid out like a fan, of the city that was expelling him—just as, according to Palou, it had expelled my parents. When he heard me he turned and came into the living room. He came and stood in the middle of the room, surrounded by furniture and paintings heaped on the floor, all wrapped in white sheets. The furnishings of the Steins' house were ghost furnishings now. Only the sea, seen through the windows, still adorned the Steins' house.

"Paula's upstairs in her room," he said. "Paula's upstairs in her room, you hear me, and I don't feel like talking."

Guillermo Stein was not smiling. Guillermo Stein was looking at me like someone looking at an uninvited guest, an unknown relative who has crossed the Atlantic and who, after the exchange of gifts and formalities, you are forced to welcome in your home for several weeks, you are forced to live with this stranger who says he's your relative but who doesn't look anything like your family, for several long, lethargic, monotonous weeks.

I left Guillermo Stein in the living room and went up to Paula Stein's room. The door was ajar.

"It's Pablo," I said, "Pablo Ridorsa, can I come in?"

"Yes, please come in," Paula replied.

Then I heard her laugh; I heard her laughter and a sudden noise and all at once my clothes were soaked with water, water was dripping down over my face and soaking my clothes. Paula Stein had put a bucket full of water over the door. A bucket that was now rolling on the floor of Paula Stein's room. I looked at her, still laughing on the mattress of her bed, and I looked at the glass boxes, the butterflies arranged by families, imprisoned by death in ether, drowned by ether and pinned on cork with silver-plated pins.

"I'm hunting elephants, Pablo, I'm hunting elephants as stupid as you and the horrible people of this city."

"Elephants never forget," I replied, "however stupid they may be, they never forget."

"Everybody here forgets, Ridorsa. Maybe you're the only one who never forgets. The others are sick, they suffer from amnesia. They live with amnesia and amnesia is what allows them to carry on living. Goodbye, Pablo Ridorsa."

Then Paula Stein got up from the bed and kissed me. She kissed my wet hair, she kissed my face and my hands. She took my face in her hands and looked at me as nobody had ever looked at me before. And it struck me that Paula Stein was crazy, that Paula Stein was completely crazy. And I ran out of her room and down the stairs and didn't say anything to Stein. I didn't say anything to anybody until I got home, where I didn't say anything either. And on my way home I walked through the area where the movie houses were and went over their names: the Rivoli, the Excelsior or, the Luxor, the Rialto, the Trocadero . . . And with their signs off, the movie houses seemed to me like abandoned graves, that afternoon when Paula Stein kissed me the movie houses seemed like the tombs of a dynasty that had been wiped off the face of the earth.

"All stand."

We all stood up at our desks when the Father Prefect entered the classroom with Stein. Father Riudavets's fanglike canines reached down to the neck of his cassock. The whiteness of Father Riudavets' canines was one with the whiteness of Father Riudavets's dog collar. Stein was carrying a little package in his hands, but he wasn't smiling, this time he wasn't smiling either.

"Sit down," Riudavets said. "You don't need to stand for us. Not this time. It's a disgrace to stand for someone like Stein even though he's with me. Sit down, we've only come to collect his things."

And Father Riudavets said "his things" as if he were saying garbage, as if he were saying we've come to collect Stein's garbage, sit down and hold your noses, I don't want you to smell bad things, I don't want to get yourselves dirty. And he was smiling, Father Riudavets was smiling triumphantly as Stein collected his things and put them in the pigskin case that had a stain shaped like the map of Africa. He was smiling as he had never smiled when he read Stein's grades and said "top honors" and looked at him as if warning him, "I'll get you one of these days, Stein, there's still time. We both have a lot of time ahead of us." And that day had arrived, the day Riudavets came to the class with his prey between his teeth: with Guillermo Stein bloody and defeated between Father Riudavets's teeth.

When Stein had collected everything, he came to my desk and left me the package he had been carrying in his hands when he came into the classroom. He didn't say goodbye to anybody. Not even me: he didn't look at me, he didn't say goodbye to me, he only left that little package wrapped in newspaper on my desk. And I hid it inside my desk, I hid it like someone hiding a shameful sin, while Riudavets and Stein left the classroom without any of us rising to our feet.

That night, after dinner, I shut myself in my room and took Stein's package from my satchel. I untied the string and unfolded the newspaper. I took Stein's gift in my hands. Stein's gift was the oval plate from his bicycle, the white porcelain plate that bore a coat of arms with unicorns and fleurs-de-lys and a motto in Latin and two black letters above the coat of arms, the two black letters CD. Stein's gift was the coat of arms of the diplomatic corps of a nation whose coat of arms did not appear in the Universal Atlas and which I now assumed was an invention of his father's. I read the Latin motto: *Respicere aliena ducet secum desgratia.* I took my dictionary from my satchel and translated the motto on my bed: "Coveting what belongs to others brings misfortune." Then I saw Stein on the first day he came to school, I saw Stein arrive with his red rain cape and his black bicycle, and I saw his colorful sweaters and his blue eyes with their copper-colored flecks, those eyes that had smiled at me as I looked at Stein's things, as I furtively watched how Stein put his things in the desk that had been assigned to him by Father Laval in the middle of the year, when the rains fell at their hardest and Guillermo Stein arrived at the school on his bicycle wearing his red rain cape.

And I put Stein's plate in the metal box where I kept my parents' postcards.

The school's assembly hall was packed. I remember it was very hot, it was always very hot in the assembly hall. On the stage, the Father Rector and the Father

Prefect, Riudavets, sat behind a table covered in red damask like military top brass in a trench, guarding the year's honors. And behind them the flag, the brown velvet flag with the shield and the coats of arms of the school. Brother Tello, standing at the microphone, was performing his ceremonial functions. Brother Tello had a steel leg that made three movements, and each of these movements had a different sound: if Brother Tello moved, in the front rows you could hear click-clack-clunk, you could hear the three sounds of Brother Tello's legs, even above the beeping of the microphone and the murmur of conversation.

We stood in the aisles, the most distinguished pupils of that year, war heroes amid a profusion of standards and blue and red banners, Carthage and Rome, laurel wreaths, ribbons, and gold, silver and bronze medals, which weren't gold, silver and bronze medals, but cast-iron medals painted gold, silver and bronze. Those for conduct were thin but solid, round crosses surrounded by laurels; those for progress were bigger and elongated, but they were empty inside and sounded like the bells on sheep when they were clipped to your shirt and clinked against each other. It was a paradox that I never understood: the Jesuits often compensated for bad conduct with the weight of their brilliant intelligence, cunning deployed for strategic purposes. Palou's natural balance, I suppose.

We had gone up onto the stage one by one, hearing our surnames followed by our first names and our success ringing out in Brother Tello's voice. Prince of history! Consul of mathematics! Magistrate of Latin! Emperor! Tribune! . . . When we got down off the stage, we were applauded as if we had come back from the German campaign. And now we stood by the entrance to the assembly hall, holding banners and standards, Romans to the right and Carthaginians to the left, the blue flag of Carthage to the left, the red SPQR to the right. And when Brother Tello's voice rang out the procession began, the procession to the stage, between the rows of seats, watched by our parents—the parents of the other pupils, I mean, because I was watched by my grandparents.

We went back up on the stage, formed two lines and stood there at the front, looking at everyone as they applauded, looking at them without seeing them, blinded by the spotlights, and with the eyes of Father Riudavets staring at our backs, Riudavets waiting like Sulla for the Ides of March, the Ides that had banished Stein. Then the first chords of the school anthem struck up and we started singing:

> *Our islands are pieces of Spain*
> *are pieces of Spain,*
> *cast out onto the sea.*
> *They are Spain's vanguards toward the Orient*

they are ships that plow
the Imperial sea . . .

And as we sang, stirred by the music, I looked for Stein in the orchestra seats; I looked for Guillermo Stein, knowing that he wasn't there; I looked for him like someone looking for the fire exit in a theater that is going up in flames, precisely because I would never again see Guillermo Stein.

That summer the Russians invaded Czechoslovakia and I was with my grandparents at Masvern. We had been invited by Uncle Federico and my grandmother had said yes. For the first time in twenty years my grandmother set foot on the land and in the house of Mavern. My grandfather was indignant at the Bolshevik tanks on the streets of Prague, but he was even more indignant at the election of Macías as president of Guinea. "Mark my words: that hottentot will have us out on our ears, I can see it all now." Uncle Federico didn't care a hoot about the streets of Prague or the thatched huts of Fernando Poo. My grandfather followed the news on my uncle's radio, which wasn't called a radio anymore, but a transistor, and looked like a cigar box wrapped in brown hide that was like cardboard with holes; it was like a box of Tuscan cigars, the kind my Uncle Federico smoked. In the loggia, my great-grandfather continued to sit with his binoculars hanging from his neck, but there were no more yachts laden with chorus girls from Berlin passing on the horizon of his eyes. In his eyes now there was only a curtain of whitish liquid and it seemed to me as if that curtain was the flag that death had planted on my great-grandfather's body. But that summer I was very happy.

That summer I received my first letter from my parents. It was my grandfather, one afternoon when, taking advantage of the fact that Uncle Federico had to visit his lawyer, he had gone down to the city, who handed me my parents' letter. My grandmother was embroidering an altar cloth for the chapel at Masvern when my grandfather waved the letter in front of my face and said, "You have a letter from London, you oaf, your parents are in London, just around the corner." The first thing I did was to look at the stamps: on one there was the profile of Queen Elizabeth, on the other one of Her Majesty's grenadiers stared up at me, a grenadier in a red uniform and a bearskin hat like the ones I cut out in the study in our house, the study at Via Portugal number 12. Then I opened it.

It was a letter written on headed paper, the paper of a hotel in Bloomsbury, the Fitzroy, I'll never forget it. You could read the name with your fingers because the letters stood out in relief: Fitzroy Hotel, Bloomsbury, London. The letter was written by my father. It was a cold, hesitant letter, with lots of beating about the bush, as if it were a letter written to a stranger to ask him for a favor. I didn't much like my father's tone in that letter. But the important thing wasn't the tone but the news that they were going to visit the island in the fall, in the middle of November. That summer I was very happy: I hunted with Uncle Federico, I played with his dogs, I fished for frogs in the stream, I swam in the circular pond at Masvern, and we went to mass in town in the Buick Roadster driven by Francisco. Everyone in the town watched us pass, sitting on the leather seats of the Buick Roadster, and Uncle Federico and my grandmother would wave at them. Uncle Federico waved exactly like Franco; the only thing missing from Uncle Federico's Buick Roadster was the Moorish Guard. And at mass we would sit in the choir stalls, next to the altar: we were the only ones to sit in the choir stalls, next to the altar, and it made me feel a little ashamed to be up there, separated from the everyone else, but I would look at my grandmother and Uncle Federico and from their faces it seemed as if they both thought this was the most natural thing in the world.

That summer I was very happy, and sitting on one of the rocking chairs in the loggia with my grandparents and my great-grandfather, I didn't know where to fit that piece of the jigsaw. I didn't know where in my life to fit the visit of my parents. I held out the letter to my grandmother, who had stopped embroidering because her hands were shaking; her hands were shaking and she had asked my grandfather to bring her the little bottle of passion flower extract, a little blue bottle my grandmother always kept in her bag, next to the bottle labeled Distovagal.

"Here you are, grandma, you keep it."

I held out the letter to her and the letter fell in the lap of her skirt and I heard Uncle Federico's voice calling me from below.

"Come on, boy, let's go and do some shooting, because there's nothing for dinner. And bring me down a cigar, I need fuel."

The sun was falling over the mountains, turning them a pinkish color, a color like the enameled face of one of those old watches in the Osiris watchmaker's shop. There was a smell of shrubs and fan palm and the sweet scent of fig and carob trees. That afternoon I shot a rabbit and two partridges. The summer was gradually fading away and my great-grandfather was fading with it. We buried him at the beginning of September. The sun shone straight down on the cemetery at Masvern. In that heat, and dressed all in black, we were like scarecrows in the sun. On the way back, Uncle Federico gave me my great-grandfather's binoculars.

"Here," he said. "Now you'll be able to see all the things my father saw."

After my great-grandfather's death, it started raining again. Summer was coming to an end and my grandparents packed their bags: it was time to go home. Uncle Federico came out to say goodbye with his black dogs that kept jumping up and down around him and that didn't scare me anymore. Uncle Federico came out to say goodbye and stood there in the lane of palm trees, the lane of the Bengal lancers, waving his riding crop as if we were leaving on a long journey. My grandparents were arguing: they couldn't agree on the mysteries of the rosary. It was the first time I heard my grandparents arguing.

And as we entered the city and Francisco moved down through the gears of my Uncle Federico's Buick Roadster, I thought about Guillermo Stein as one thinks about a shadow; I realized that I didn't know anything about Guillermo Stein, that neither Planas nor Palou, even though they thought they did, ever really found out anything about Stein; and then it struck me that maybe life was like that, not knowing anything about anybody: not knowing anything about anybody, or even about ourselves, but living as if we did.

My grandparents were still arguing.

3

When we got back from Masvern at the end of September, a postcard from Paula Stein was waiting for me. I'm now married to her.

Her brother Guillermo died in a Palestinian terrorist attack at Fiumicino airport in Rome in 1973. He was seventeen years old.

I never discovered what Guillermo Stein was doing in Rome.

ABOUT THE AUTHOR

José Carlos Llop is the author of the novels *La cámara de ámbar* (Muchnick, 1996; finalist Prix Jean Monnet de Littérature Européenne 2011), *El informe Stein* (Muchnik, 1995 / RBA, 2008; Prix Écureuil de Littérature Étrangère 2008), *Háblame del tercer hombre* (Muchnik, 2001 / RBA, 2011), *El mensajero de Argel* (Destino, 2005) and *París: suite 1940* (RBA, 2007).

He has also written two books of short stories, *Pasaporte diplomático* (El Aleph, 1991) and *La novela del siglo* (NH Award for the Best Book of Short Stories 1999, El Aleph, 1999). He has published nine books of poetry and is the author of five volumes of diaries.

His latest works are *En la ciudad sumergida* (RBA, 2010), an essay on Mallorca that got the Special Mention by the Jury of the 2013 Prix Méditerranée Étranger, and *Solsticio* (RBA, 2013).

ABOUT THE TRANSLATOR

HOWARD CURTIS lives and works in London, England. He has translated many books from Spanish, French and Italian, mostly of contemporary fiction, and has won a number of prizes for his translations. Spanish-language writers he has translated include Luis Sepúlveda, Francisco Coloane and Santiago Gamboa.

Lightning Source UK Ltd.
Milton Keynes UK
UKOW04f2156010515

250759UK00003B/3/P